PINK MOON RISING

A Paranormal Cozy Mystery

VELLA DAY

Erotic Reads Publishing

A Witch's Cove Mystery
Book 18
Copyright © 2022 Vella Day

www.velladay.com

velladayauthor@gmail.com

Cover Art by Jaycee DeLorenzo

Edited by Rebecca Cartee

Published in the United States of America

E-book ISBN: 978-1-951430-46-7

Print book ISBN: 978-1-951430-47-4

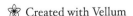 Created with Vellum

ABOUT THE BOOK

A movie production in Witch's Cove, a talking bad boy raccoon, and a dead leading lady. Just your typical day in paradise.

Hi, I'm Glinda Goodall, and I am so excited that I am going to be in a movie! So what if it's not much of a speaking part. Just being around celebrities will be awesome. Or at least it was until one of the leading ladies turned up dead.

It's not that my fiancé and partner in The Pink Iguana Sleuths and I aren't used to dead bodies, this case also included a raccoon, who happened to be the leading lady's familiar. It wouldn't be so bad if he hadn't recruited Iggy for his nocturnal misadventures.

Since we suspected magic had something to do with the woman's death, the sheriff actually welcomed our interference (his word, not mine). With a large cast, the suspect list was endless. As daunting as that sounds, between the gossip queens in town and several powerful beings, I'm confident we'll find the killer.

If you want to check up on Iggy and this miscreant raccoon, head to the alley behind our strip mall, and you might catch a glimpse of them. They would be happy to fill you in on the latest news.

CHAPTER ONE

"HOW DID THE SHOOT GO TODAY?" I asked my long-time girlfriend, Penny Carsted.

Hi, I'm Glinda Goodall, and I've lived in Witch's Cove, Florida my whole life. Penny and I had waitressed together for three years at my Aunt Fern's restaurant, the Tiki Hut Grill. While she was still working there, I had moved on to running The Pink Iguana Sleuths with my fiancé, Jaxson Harrison.

Did I regret changing professions? Not at all, except that waitressing brought in more money—at least in the beginning it did. Being amateur sleuths, Jaxson and I worked for free unless the client wanted to reward us, which was what happened big time a year ago. We actually received enough money to buy the strip mall across the street, which we use as our source of income.

And speaking of that series of stores, we were currently renting out what used to be the music store to a Canadian movie company who was using it as a set for a diner. Apparently, the director liked the front and side windows of the shop since it showcased our beach town.

"The shoot was good," Penny said. "I had a scene with the doctor today. Let me tell you that I'm so happy I don't have a real broken ankle. Wearing that boot for a few hours is a pain. Literally. I can't imagine wearing a plaster cast."

Penny and I were hired as extras for the Pink Moon Rising Productions movie, *No Love Potion Needed*. In it, I played a waitress at Sampson's diner where one of the two leading ladies also worked. Penny's character was a frequent patient for the new-in-town hot doctor, Ivan Maynard. Because of her *injury*, she needed many appointments. So far, Penny had not complained about having to be in the same room as him.

"How was Dr. Hottie today?" That was her nickname for the leading man, not mine. I only had eyes for Jaxson.

Even though Penny was practically engaged, she had no problem looking. "He bungled a few lines today, and the director came down hard on him. I felt sorry for Samuel, but he was kind of rude back."

"That's not good."

"No, but he is the one with all the movie awards. It's his name that will bring in the viewers, and he knows it."

That was an interesting take. "I rarely interact with him. All I know is that the woman who plays Gloria Vega—the doctor's main love interest—doesn't think he has any flaws—or rather the character she plays thinks he's amazing."

Bethany, who plays Gloria, also waitressed at the same diner where I *worked*. She told me that when the new doctor arrived in town, her character set her sights on him. She thought he really liked her until he hired a nurse who was a real witch. Later on in the movie, we would find out that the nurse put a love spell on him. I'd say more, but we are only given the script a day or two in advance, and Bethany wouldn't say anything else because of her non-disclosure agreement. Whatever.

Penny sipped her wine. We were having a much-needed girls' night out, opting to stay in at my one-bedroom apartment this evening since it was quiet and confidential.

"I wish I could watch more of the movie being made," Penny said. "It really is exciting, but I'm not around much when the two actors who play Dr. Maynard and Gloria have their scenes, which is sad because that's why I agreed to be in the movie in the first place. I wanted to see them act."

"I hear you."

"You know what bugs me the most?" she asked, though I suspected she wasn't interested in my answer.

"What?"

"The director films things out of order so I can't tell what's really going on in the story. Not only that, I have a day job, and I can't just sit around all day and watch."

"Like me?" I grinned. "Thankfully, Jaxson and I don't have any clients at the moment, so I can hang out a bit more than you."

"Do you think you'll ever do something like this again?" Penny asked.

"Maybe, but only if I have more than ten speaking lines. Even though I play a waitress, no one is allowed to eat the food, and that's just wrong, not to mention wasteful. All I ever do is ask if the person wants more coffee or any dessert."

"I bet Dolly will be sad to see the movie end," she said.

Dolly Andrews—one of the best town gossips and owner of the Spellbound Diner—made the food that the movie set diner pretended to serve.

The cat door flapped open, and in waddled my

nine-pound iguana—make that my talking pink iguana. Iggy was my familiar and was quite the character. "Where have you been?" I asked.

"With Bandit."

Ah, yes, Bandit. He was a twenty-pound bad boy raccoon who was the familiar of the actor who played the character Alexa. Because Janet was one of the stars of the movie, the director allowed her to have her raccoon with her. I talked to Bandit on occasion, but I pretended as if I didn't understand his response. I'm sure Iggy already told him that I was faking it.

"What were you two up to?" I asked.

"It was so cool." He looked over at Penny. "Oh, hey. Nice to see you."

Wasn't he Mr. Polite when others were around?

"Hey, Iggy."

My familiar went over to my friend, probably for some attention. When he came near us, I held up a hand. "Hold up right there, mister. You kind of stink. What did you get into?"

"Bandit showed me how to open garbage cans. Do you know he can open locks too? His hands are just like humans—well almost."

"You can't do that, can you?" Iggy's fingers were thin and a bit too flexible.

"No. I don't have strong fingers like Bandit does."

"Where were you two while he was showing you all of this tomfoolery?"

"Near the trailer of the guy who plays Dr. Maynard. There's a trash can next to his place. Bandit doesn't like him, which is why he wanted to see if he could tip over the can."

"Why doesn't he like the actor?" I asked. I didn't comment on the fact that Iggy didn't weigh enough to tip anything over.

"Do you have anything I can eat?" Iggy asked, not answering my question. "Bandit eats anything and everything. He's kind of like the seagulls, except that he makes the mess instead of cleaning it up—well sort of cleaning it up. They just eat the leftover food. But Bandit is better in that he can talk, and he doesn't poop on me."

I chuckled. My poor familiar had an ongoing war with the seagulls at the beach. Iggy truly believed that Tippy, one of the many seagulls, had it in for him.

"Sure. I'll fix you some lettuce." I turned to Penny. "Be right back."

While I went into the kitchen, she and Iggy chatted about his new friend. She also asked him about his best friend, Hugo, but Iggy refused to discuss it. I hope those two hadn't had a falling out.

I fixed Iggy a plate and carried it out. "Here you go. Eat and then it's bath time for you."

"Okay."

Iggy loved water, but he said I was often too rough with the washcloth. I wouldn't have to resort to such measures if he stayed away from filth.

"Are you working tomorrow?" I asked Penny.

"Only at the restaurant, so you won't see me hobbling around the set. Besides, I just had a *check-up* with Dr. Maynard, so I'm not sure when I'm supposed to go back. I think my character has a crush on him. Why else would she keep making up excuses to see him?"

"I think your character definitely has a thing for Dr. Maynard. I am due on set at nine," I grumbled.

Penny winced. "That's really early for you."

Normally, I slept in until ten or later. "Yeah, but the movie won't last forever."

"True." She finished her glass of wine. "Since I have the breakfast shift, I need to be going. Say hi to Jaxson for me."

I smiled. "I will."

After we hugged goodbye, Penny left. Once Iggy finished eating, I lifted him up. "Time to get clean, Mister Stinky."

"I need to tell Bandit that garbage cans are off limits from now on."

I swallowed a smile. "You do that."

The next morning, I'd just placed some delicious smelling food in front of two actors when the director yelled, "Cut."

I hoped I hadn't been the one to mess up. In case I was, I backed up, though what good that would do, I didn't know. The fake diner only had two booths that were situated next to the window and five tables that were spread out in the rest of the small area. The counter was along the back wall, with the former back room serving as the fake kitchen. There weren't a lot of places to hide—or any for that matter.

Bethany looked over at the rest of the cast and then turned to Shawn Shields, the producer/director. "What's wrong?" she asked.

Shawn was about forty-five, kind of pudgy, and had a beard in need of trimming.

"Where is Janet? She's supposed to be here." The director sounded rather impatient.

Janet was the woman who played Nurse Alexa Brown. Since I wasn't in charge of anyone, I relaxed. I'd heard that Janet was not always reliable, but this was the first time I'd heard that she'd missed being the center of attention.

Chris Pena, the screenwriter for the movie, leaned close to the director. I'd say Chris was probably the same age as Shawn, but he was tall, rather thin, and much better looking.

"You. Need. To. Do. Something. About. Her," Chris ground out.

From what I've read, except for a few really big movies, the screenwriter never had a say in what went on during the production. I guess this guy was either too big to say no to, or he helped finance this rather small budget movie. On the other hand, these two could be dating.

"I will—or rather, I wish I could."

What did that mean? I was surprised the director didn't keep his voice down.

I looked out the window toward the park to see if Janet was on her way over to the set. Only the three main characters merited a trailer. The rest of the cast was staying at the Magic Wand Hotel, which was located down the street—just on the other side of our strip mall.

I was happy for the hotel owners that they'd be booked up for a few months, but they probably would have been full this time of year anyway. It was high season, after all.

Wherever Janet was at the moment, I hoped she showed up soon.

"Chuck, go find her," the director barked out.

"Where do you suggest I look?" his assistant asked.

The director rolled his eyes. "See if she's at the hotel doing makeup—at least she should be there."

"And if she's not?"

Chris Pena placed a hand on the director's arm. "She might be with Samuel somewhere." He raised his eyebrows, but I didn't know what that meant. "They have a big scene coming up. I'll check both of their trailers."

"Good." The director turned to Chuck. "What are you waiting for? Go." He then faced the rest of us. "Take five everyone, but stay here."

This was the part of the movie process I found the most distasteful—the standing around. Since it was impossible to know how much time a scene required, Janet might have decided to arrive on her own schedule. Waiting might not be her thing either.

The movie had only been shooting for a couple of weeks, but during that time, I had the sense that she thought she was someone special. Considering she could have her *pet* raccoon with her, Janet might be right.

The rather sour and fastidious screenwriter rushed across the street to the park. There were four trailers on the near edge of the park. Three for the main actors and one for the director.

Chris went to the one on the far left that belonged to Dr. Hottie. He knocked, and a few seconds later, the actor who portrayed the doctor opened up. Being across the street, I couldn't hear anything. Even if I had the ability to cloak myself and teleport, like a few entities I knew could, it would look a tad odd if I just disappeared from the diner.

Apparently, Janet wasn't there, because Chris then went next door to her trailer. He knocked, but I didn't see her open up. Either the door was unlocked or she told him to enter, because Chris went inside. I walked over to an empty booth and sat down. I imagined it would take her a while to get ready and come out.

Another cast member joined me. "There should be a penalty every time you miss your call," Lynn Lurch said.

"Wouldn't that be nice?"

Two minutes later, Chris burst into our fake diner, his face flushed. "I can't believe it. Janet is dead!"

The director jumped up. "What? Did you call 9-1-1?"

"Why? She's dead."

"How do you know?" He waved a hand. "We still need to call the cops!"

"Sorry."

Not trusting Chris to pull it together in this tragic moment, I slipped my phone out of the pocket and called the sheriff's office. Pearl Dillsmith, the receptionist and the sheriff's grandmother, answered the call, but this time I didn't start with my usual friendly greeting.

"Pearl, it's Glinda. One of the cast members is dead. Where's Steve?" I refrained from saying she was murdered, but that was what I was thinking—unless she'd taken her own life.

"He's here. Where are you?"

"I'm at the fake diner." We hadn't come up with a better name for it. "Janet is in her trailer. It's the middle one."

"I'll send Steve right over."

"Thank you."

So much for my movie debut.

CHAPTER TWO

I COULDN'T BELIEVE one of the headliners was dead! I didn't know the actress, Janet, all that well, other than she was a witch who had a raccoon for a familiar. Now what would happen to Bandit? I hadn't had a problem finding a home for Ruby, the white cat whose owner was a big contributor to Witch's Cove, but a raccoon who liked to forage through garbage and get into trouble would be a hard sell. Unfortunately, familiars weren't like ordinary animals. He wouldn't do well in the wild or with other non-magical raccoons.

Sheriff Steve Rocker and his deputy, Nash Solana, rushed past the set and headed to the park.

"Chris, stop pacing," the director said. "Come sit down and tell me again what you saw. Calmer this time."

The distraught man did as he was requested, but he planted his elbows on his knees and buried his head in his hands instead of giving details. "How can she be dead?" he wailed.

Each of the main stars had understudies, but it would require every scene that Janet had been in to be reshot. I had no idea how much work or money that would entail—or if the studio would want to continue making the movie.

The actress who was sitting at my booth almost looked scared. "Who would do this to her?" Lynn asked. "Or do you think she like...overdosed?"

I hadn't thought along those lines. "Did you hear that Janet was into drugs?" I wasn't so naïve to think illegal substances couldn't be found in our town, but I wasn't aware we had a big problem. It was also possible, she brought the drugs with her.

"No, but what else could it be? Heart failure?"

I studied Lynn. She was slightly younger than me, quite pretty and seemingly innocent. "Maybe someone killed her." I kept my voice to a near whisper.

"Murdered?" Her voice rose.

"Shh. Who knows? Maybe. Janet was what? Thirty or a little bit older?"

Lynn shrugged. "Probably."

My sleuth brain shot into high gear. "Did you see her argue with anyone?"

"Not really, but the actress who played Gloria didn't seem to like her," Lynn said.

"I think that is part of her role. Gloria is supposed to be in love with Dr. Maynard, and then Nurse Alexa steals his heart—via a love potion." Why the movie was called *No Love Potion Needed* was still unclear.

Lynn nodded. "That's true." She leaned closer. "I saw Samuel get in a squabble with Janet because of her rodent."

"Bandit is a raccoon, not a rodent."

Lynn waved a hand. "Whatever. I heard the animal somehow got into his trailer and trashed the place."

I hadn't heard that. "When was this?"

"In the beginning of the shoot."

That was before I was hired. "The actor should take it up with the director. I don't see Samuel killing anyone over an animal who'd gone rogue, do you?"

"I suppose not."

If anything, he'd try to do away with Bandit, not his owner. I looked over at Shawn Shields who was attempting to console the screenwriter. "I had no idea that Chris cared that much about Janet. He always seemed so angry that she wasn't saying the lines like he wrote them." I kept my voice soft. The room was rather small, which meant my voice would travel.

"I think he's just in shock at having found her body. Have you ever seen a dead person before?" she asked.

All the time. "My parents run the funeral home in town. I'm kind of used to it."

Lynn shivered. "I never would be."

About thirty minutes later, I nodded to the park. "Looks like our medical examiner is on top of things."

Lynn looked over and watched in fascination as two of Dr. Sanchez's workers loaded the body into her van. Steve and Nash would be processing the scene for a while. I'm sure he'd insist that no one enter the trailer for any reason until the case was solved or until they'd finished with the interior. He also would make sure that all of the actors remained in town, though if shooting were to continue, it wouldn't be a problem.

Shawn Shields stood. "I think we have to call it a wrap for today people. I've jotted down who is here just in case you need an alibi."

An alibi? That kind of implied murder. Did he know something about Janet's death—as in she'd died in the last few minutes while we were all here? I, however, wasn't going to mention that. And the director didn't have to tell me twice that I could leave.

After I said goodbye to Lynn, I took off. I was rather curious to know if Iggy's raccoon friend had seen anything.

I rushed across the street and half jogged up the steps to our second-story office. Thankfully, Jaxson was there. My cousin, Rihanna, wasn't back from her afternoon college classes yet, but I was sure she'd be interested in every detail when she returned home. Rihanna had moved to Witch's Cove a year and a half ago and moved into the spare room in the office. She'd helped with most of our cases since then.

Jaxson looked up. "You finished shooting for the day?"

"No. Well, yes, but only because Janet is dead."

"What?"

I probably shouldn't have led with that, but by now, finding a dead body—or hearing of one—wasn't all that unusual for us. "Let me get a drink, and I'll fill you in."

As soon as I stepped into the kitchen, Iggy followed me in. "Janet is dead?"

"I'm afraid so."

"What's going to happen to Bandit?"

I was happy Iggy had developed empathy for his new friend. "I don't know." I poured myself an iced tea. "Maybe you can find out from Bandit if Janet had a bad heart or something."

Iggy backed away. "I'm not telling him she died."

That would be hard. "Someone has to."

"You can do it."

"Once we know more, maybe I will. Or the sheriff can tell him."

Iggy shook his head. "I don't know if he can understand Bandit."

I'd put a spell on Steve—and tried to include Nash—to allow him to understand Iggy and some other familiars. Steve had never said his ability had worn off. "Are you guessing, or do you know that Steve can't understand you?"

"Guessing."

I carried my drink into the living room and sat down next to Jaxson, who was in his usual spot at the computer. Since we didn't have a case, he was working on one of his own hobbies.

He spun to face me. "Tell me what happened."

I told him about Janet not showing up to the set. "The director had his assistant check the makeup room at the hotel, and the screenwriter said he'd check the trailers. He thought that Janet might be rehearsing her lines with Samuel."

Jaxson pressed his lips together. "In that case, if Steve and Nash are processing the scene, and if Elissa is autopsying the body, there is little we can do until we find out the cause of death."

Jaxson was always so logical. "I know, but I don't like sitting around."

He smiled. "I'm sure by lunchtime, the whole town will have heard what happened—and probably have a few theories too."

He was right about that, assuming the sheriff had concluded anything by then. I tapped the table. "I think I'll ask Genevieve to do a little reconnaissance."

Our gargoyle shifter could not only teleport, she could remain invisible—and those were just two of her many talents.

Jaxson chuckled. "You are incorrigible. What if Steve or Nash bumps into her. It's not like Genevieve is like a puff of smoke. She might be able to cloak herself, but she's still solid."

"Your logic could punch holes in a piece of steel."

He grinned. "Then how about a shake at the diner instead? We can fill Dolly in on what happened. Maybe she can give her good friend, Pearl, a call."

The tension whooshed out of my body. "That is a brilliant idea." I turned to Iggy. "Do you want to come with us?"

"No. I think I should find Bandit. He'll need support when he learns of his host's death. When he sees the sheriff's department in Janet's trailer, he'll know something is up."

"That's very kind of you."

"I think so too."

So much for being humble. It only took a few minutes to reach Dolly's diner. I hoped someone let her know that the movie would be delayed a bit because of the death of one of the movie's stars. That would mean, she didn't need to supply the food for a while.

Sadly, I didn't know a lot about Janet, like whether she was married, or even where she was from. In my mind, the characters were real people. That might make finding a motive more difficult, assuming it was murder.

Because all of the diner booths were taken, we opted to sit at the counter. I couldn't remember the last time we sat there.

Dolly smiled briefly. The poor lady was really swamped, but she lifted a finger to indicate she'd be over in a minute.

I leaned closer to Jaxson. "Do you think she might know about Janet already?" It was possible Steve told his grandmother what had happened.

"I couldn't say, but I'm sure you'll bring her up to speed in no time."

"Funny man. I don't know much, but hopefully

·she'll call her gossipy friend while we are having our shakes and find out more."

Two minutes later, Dolly rushed over. "Sorry about that. The place is hopping."

"We can see that." January was always a big time for our town. "Did you hear what happened to one of the main characters in the movie?"

"No! What?"

Pearl must not know anything then. Otherwise, she would have called already. "Janet, who plays the character Alexa Brown, is dead. We don't know if it was murder, suicide, or death by natural causes."

Dolly sucked in a breath. "Wasn't Alexa the doctor's nurse?"

She had been paying attention. "Yes."

"She was so young. Do you know what happened? Like when she died, and who found her?"

I filled her in with the few facts I had. "I hope you'll keep your ears open."

"Oh, you can bet your bottom dollar I will. No one has contacted me about stopping the food delivery though."

"Really? Most likely Shawn and his assistant were a tad preoccupied and hadn't thought to contact you. I'm sure they will." Or so I hoped.

"How long before they resume production?" she asked.

"I have no idea what his plans are, but I'm thinking he won't need the food for a few days, but I could be wrong."

"He's probably adhering to the old adage, *the show must go on*," Dolly said.

"I wouldn't be surprised."

Another customer called her name. "What can I get you two?"

I ordered a chocolate shake, and Jaxson went with a black coffee. Dolly didn't even write it down. She just rushed off to help the other customer, but I knew she'd fill our order as soon as she could.

"I guess we have to wait until Elissa finishes the autopsy," I said.

"Are you hoping it's murder?" Jaxson asked.

Was I? Janet was dead. How she died wasn't going to change that. "Maybe."

Jaxson smiled. "That's my favorite sleuth. I'm glad you're doing what you love."

"I am. And I am with someone I love, too."

His eyes widened. "The *L* word. Nice."

I punched him lightly. "Change of subject. What should we do with Bandit?"

"One thing is for sure, we are not having a raccoon at our office."

I held up my hand. "I couldn't agree more, but we can't let animal services take Bandit either."

"What are you proposing?"

"Let's hope that Janet has family who is willing to care for him."

Jaxson lowered his chin. "We can only hope. You know that Iggy will try to convince you to keep him, right?"

"I know."

"We have to stay strong and tell him no."

Of course, Jaxson was right. "I'll try."

He smiled. "Good."

Dolly delivered our drinks a few minutes later. "Promise me that as soon as you hear anything that you let me know, okay?" she asked.

"Sure, and you do the same," I shot back.

"You can count on it." Dolly flashed us a smile and then went back to her busy diner.

Jaxson sipped his steaming coffee. "If you had to guess, who would you say might have killed Janet—assuming it was murder?"

"Sadly, I don't know these people very well. They are really good actors, and as such, they'd have a different relationship with Nurse Alexa than with Janet, the woman who played the nurse. The character, Gloria Vega, was supposed to hate Alexa, but when the actress and I interacted, she was sweet."

He wrapped his hands around his cup and looked off to the side. "That will make it a lot harder. Character Gloria might want to kill character Alexa, but the two actresses could be best friends off set, for all we know."

"I'm afraid so. It's not like I hang around the set all day long either. I'm mostly in the fake diner. I see Gloria, or rather Bethany, while I'm there, but not often when she has a scene with Samuel—the man her character wants."

"Let's hope that the autopsy provides answers."

"Fingers crossed."

CHAPTER THREE

AFTER TWO LONG days without any leaked information or any movie work, I was at the office—because I didn't want to be anywhere else—when my cell rang. "It's Elissa," I told Jaxson. "Hurray! We might finally learn something."

"Why would the medical examiner be calling you? We haven't heard she'd filed her final report, have we?"

"No, but her calling me isn't that big of a surprise. Maybe she thinks magic is involved and needs me." My pulse rose at the prospect.

He pointed a finger at me. "True, but you won't find out unless you answer the phone."

Whoops. "Hey, Elissa."

"Oh, Glinda. Could I borrow you and your magical pink pendant for a bit?"

I pumped a fist. I loved trying to find out the cause of death when the medical examiner was stumped. "Sure. When would be a good time for me to stop over?"

"Now?"

"I'll be right there." It wasn't as if I had anything better to do. Besides, I'd be the first to hear what caused the woman's death—or what Elissa Sanchez believed the victim died from.

"Good luck," Jaxson said.

"Thank you. Do you want to come?"

He chuckled. "That would be a no."

"You sound like Iggy. Speaking of which, where is he?"

"I think he said he wanted to be with Bandit in his *time of need*," Jaxson said.

Janet's death had occurred two days ago, but I totally understood that grief didn't have a time limit. "I thought Bandit was nocturnal."

Jaxson shrugged. "He is, kind of. I think he is often up at night because he believes he can get away with more stuff at that time, not because his body tells him he should be awake. According to Iggy, Bandit has habits that are different from ordinary raccoons."

"Good to know. I was hoping with Janet gone that Bandit would settle down and not cause mischief all the time, in part because I was hoping that Iggy would try to help him embrace a more straight-and-narrow path."

My fiancé grinned. "Good luck with that."

I kissed his cheek and then headed out to the morgue. Because it was quite cool out, I thought I'd walk so I could enjoy the Florida winter day. Our cool season was short-lived, and I liked to take advantage of it when I could.

Out of habit, I checked the walkway over the street that Iggy used to cross the road.

"What the..." I walked over to the monkey bridge where Iggy and Bandit were perched. My familiar was watching Bandit throw food at the cars below. I bet if Iggy had been able to reach over the green mesh side barrier, he would have participated. Even if he tried, though, I doubt his aim would be good.

This bad behavior had to stop. I realize that Bandit was hurting emotionally—or at least Iggy claimed he was—but tormenting drivers could prove to be dangerous. I pressed the button to cross the street. As soon as the light turned red, I rushed to the middle of the street and looked up.

"Hey, Glinda," Iggy said, sounding totally innocent.

"Would you come down please? And Bandit too."

"Why?" Iggy didn't disobey me very often.

"Because throwing food at cars could cause an accident. Not to mention your weight, combined with Bandit's, might result in the bridge collapsing."

I had taken several physics classes in college, and I was pretty sure it could support both of them, but I needed to give Iggy a reason to come down.

"You're no fun," Iggy said. My iguana waddled across the swinging bridge toward the office, while Bandit headed in the opposite direction.

I wanted to call out to the raccoon familiar and ask him to come over to our side so I could speak with him about proper behavior in our town, but I wasn't his host. Nor did I think he'd listen to me.

Since the light was about to turn red, I hurried back to the sidewalk and waited for Iggy to climb down. As soon as he was within reach, I plucked him off the tree. "I wish you wouldn't encourage him."

"Me? Encourage him? Give me a break. Bandit thought of it on his own. Besides, he's upset over Janet's death and needs my support."

"You could have told him not to engage in such destructive behavior."

"And chance losing a friend? It's not like I have a lot of them, you know."

That was a tough life choice. "I get it. I do, but how about suggesting that he vent his frustration in another way?"

"What way is that?" Iggy asked, sounding rather defiant.

"You two could snoop around to see if you hear anything about what might have happened to Bandit's host."

"You really want us to snoop?"

"Sure. Why not?" I suppose if they were going to be together, they might as well be useful. "I'm headed to the morgue to see what might have caused Janet's death. Bandit doesn't know how she died, does he?"

"No. He said a lot of people were in and out of her trailer all the time. He didn't like that. Janet had basically ignored him the whole time they were here."

An absurd yet horrible idea struck. "Bandit didn't have anything to do with her death, did he?"

"Are you kidding? No! He's a great guy."

What was he talking about? "Bandit causes problems. I don't like you being around him so much." I probably shouldn't have let my issues pour out like that, but I worried about Iggy.

"I'm sixteen years old. I can hang out with who I want to." He lifted his chest.

"Is that right? Well, I'm twenty-eight, and I don't have to feed or house you if I don't want to." I was kidding, of course, but I wasn't going to be manipulated by a nine-pound iguana. It didn't matter that he was adorably cute.

"You wouldn't dare."

I didn't want to get into this right now. I had a dead body to work on. I walked him back to the office and then set him down on the handrail. "Please go upstairs and think about how you—and probably Bandit—can contribute to helping find out what happened to Janet instead of causing more problems and diverting everyone's energy away from this tragedy."

He looked back at me and then raced up to the office. Sheesh. Iggy never acted like this before Bandit came on the scene. I was hoping Jaxson could talk some sense into my familiar just as soon as I told him what happened.

Since Elissa was expecting me, I rushed down the street to the morgue. When I entered, she was in the main area. "I'm sorry I'm late," I said. "I had to take care of some juvenile antics."

"No problem. Iggy acting up?"

"Yes. He has a new friend who is a bad influence on him."

"Maybe if we can find a way to involve Iggy in the case, he'll forget all about this new friend."

"Wouldn't that be nice?" I saw no need to tell her about Bandit's abilities or his antics.

"Come into the back," she said.

Lying on the slab with a sheet up to her neck, was

Janet who looked rather peaceful. "No blunt force trauma or poison in her system, I take it?"

"No. I'll tell you more once you've done your magic on her."

That was for the best. I didn't want to know anything that might affect my conclusion. I removed my necklace and then stepped over to the body. "She is so young."

Even though Janet was only a few years older than me, in death, she appeared younger and a lot paler. As was my usual practice, I started at her feet and worked my way upward. Swinging my pendant back and forth, I waited for my pink diamond to change color. Green would signal a blockage of some sort— like a heart attack. Considering her age, I doubted I'd see that color, but I would keep an open mind. Purple was for poison, but Elissa said she hadn't found any in Janet's system. Yellow, green, and blue all represented other ailments.

I carefully swung the pendant over her entire body, but the stone didn't do anything until I reached her head. Then it changed to a bright yellow.

I stilled. "Magic."

"So it appears. Any idea what kind?" Elissa asked.

Even if the stone had turned purple, I wouldn't have been able to narrow down the type of poison, and it was the same with magic. That meant I couldn't tell anything about the nature of the spell that was used on poor Janet. "I'm afraid not, but we know the killer was either a witch or a warlock."

"You know I can't put that in the report." Elissa appeared frustrated.

"What did you find out? That might help me narrow things down."

She pressed her lips together, probably trying to decide how much to reveal. This was an on-going investigation, after all. "I've never seen anything like this before. The blood in her brain was practically gone."

Visions of vampires raced through my head, though I always pictured those mythical characters as draining the blood from the whole body. "I trust there were no puncture wounds anywhere? Or wouldn't the person need to do that?" My knowledge of physiology was sorely lacking.

"No puncture wounds, and since there were no drugs in her system, I can't put the pieces together. I measured the blood taken, and she had less than she should have. It was as if the blood evaporated. Medically speaking, that's not possible."

I looked over at the dead woman. It was no wonder she was so pale. "Could the person have been able to remove the blood from her body after she died?"

"I won't go into the details of how that would be next to impossible without any signs, so let's focus on how a warlock or witch could have done this."

"Okay. When did she die?" I asked.

"About twelve or fourteen hours before she was found."

I did some math in my head. "Between eight and ten last night then."

"Yes."

"Did you know that Janet was a witch, and that she has a familiar who is a talking raccoon?"

She studied me for a moment, probably trying to decide if I was telling the truth or pulling her leg. "No, I didn't. Is that important?"

"Raccoons in general are nocturnal, even though Bandit has no problem adapting to our time. I'm hoping he heard something when she died. Few people will even think that a raccoon or any familiar can speak." So what if Iggy claimed Bandit didn't know anything.

"That's good. Talk to him."

"I will. I'll also check with Levy Poole to see what he and his coven can come up with regarding a spell that kills and affects the brain."

"Great. Let me know."

"For sure." Even if Levy found the exact spell, I doubt Elissa could put that as the cause of death. I hope our talented medical examiner could come up with something that sounded scientific.

Levy had helped Elissa in the past and had been instrumental in finding spells for me. After we discussed how Elissa's son was doing in school, I left. I might have considered talking with the gossip queens, but if Elissa hadn't turned in the autopsy report yet, Steve wouldn't know much. And if the sheriff wasn't up to speed, then the gossip wouldn't be flowing.

On my way back to the office, I called Levy.

"Glinda, Glinda. How is my favorite witch sleuth?"

I chuckled. All I did was cause him problems. "I have a stumper for you today."

"My favorite kind. Tell me about it."

I told him that one of the stars on the movie set where I worked had died. "She was maybe thirty, so I'm thinking someone murdered her. Okay, I'm virtually certain it was murder, because my pink pendant indicated magic was present at her death."

"I see. And Dr. Sanchez? What did she conclude?"

"She can't figure it out either, which was why she called me in and asked me to use my pendant on the body. Considering it's impossible to have little blood in the brain when it was present everywhere else,

Elissa agrees it must have been the work of a witch or warlock."

"What can I do to help?" he asked.

"Find a spell that could cause this. We'd both like to know how removing blood is even possible."

"Remember when I removed a powerful warlock's abilities?"

That was a long time ago. "Sure. Are you saying it's like that?"

"I'm saying that not every warlock needs a spell. But even if they do, they might not know how it works."

Okay, that didn't help. "So you've never heard of anything like this before?"

"No, but I will check into it. It might take a day or two."

"Any guidance would be welcome."

"You bet," he said.

I disconnected and continued to the office. By now, Rihanna should be back from her classes, and I sure could use her insight. I also could use a few other people's opinions, but it might be best not to involve the whole town at this stage of the investigation. Information had a way of leaking out.

Inside, I found two of my favorite people—or rather three, if I counted Iggy.

"How did it go?" Jaxson asked.

"It was strange."

Iggy came up to me. "Seriously?"

I looked down at him. "Seriously, what?"

"You didn't shower, did you?"

Uh-oh. "I forgot. Would you like me to?"

"Does a seagull poop?"

Whenever I spent time in the morgue, the smell of death permeated my clothes, offending Iggy to the max. "Fine, I'll be right back."

"Hold on. You can't leave us hanging like that," Rihanna said. "Jaxson filled me in, but I want to know what your necklace revealed? Was this woman murdered?"

"Yes. Janet was murdered by someone with magic. That's all we know." I didn't want to give Iggy nightmares by telling him her condition at death.

"Did you call Levy?" Rihanna asked.

"I did. Let me clean up, and we can take it from there."

"I'll prepare your white board," my nineteen-year-old cousin said.

I smiled. "I knew there was a reason why I keep you around."

If she'd had something nearby, I bet she would have thrown it at me. She grinned. "You'll pay for that."

CHAPTER FOUR

"I THINK we should find out all of the cast members' full names," Jaxson said once I had returned from cleaning up. "You never know who these actors might be."

"Are you thinking one of them has killed before? Before you answer, even if they have, there wouldn't be a record of it since they are acting in the movie instead of sitting in prison."

He nodded. "I'd still like to do a search. If Steve has a suspect, I'd like to do a deep dive on him or her."

"Great. I'll see what I can find out."

Iggy waddled over to the sofa and climbed onto the coffee table. That move meant he wanted to share some of his brilliance with the peasants.

"Yes, Detective Iggy?"

"Bandit and I were discussing what might have happened to Janet."

"Do tell."

"Janet had gotten a hold of the book that the movie is based on."

"I've heard a lot of actors like to read the story beforehand to get a feel for their character."

"Sure, but apparently, Janet found out that her character was going to be killed off. I guess no one told her."

That seemed odd. I thought actors were always sent the script beforehand. How else would they know if they wanted to accept the role?

"Maybe Chris changed the script." I sat down on the sofa, and Jaxson wheeled over his desk chair. "You said that in the book, a character was going to kill Nurse Alexa? Which one?"

Killing off a character had little to do with what happened in real life, but Iggy not realize that.

"Gloria. Why her you might ask? She really liked the doctor and thought that Nurse Alexa was in the way."

"Gloria Vega—or rather Bethany—the woman I work with in the diner, is the murderer?" Her character was so sweet.

"Yup."

"How did she kill Nurse Alexa?" Jaxson asked.

"She used a spell."

Something was off. "Bethany is playing a witch?"

Iggy dropped down onto his belly. "Yes, and news flash: she is a witch in real life too. Don't you people talk to each other?"

You people? "Not always. Witches don't go around announcing something like that—especially if they didn't grow up in Witch's Cove. But tell me, how did you learn that Bethany has magical abilities? Did you see her do a spell?" Though I don't know when he could have. Bethany worked really long hours.

"I don't know firsthand, but that's what Bandit told me."

And the raccoon would never lie, right? "Okay, let's go with Bethany being a witch. Considering a real witch killed Janet, maybe Bethany is the killer. Did Bandit say anything else?" I asked.

"Nothing other than Bethany didn't like Janet," he said.

"Are you talking about the characters in the movie, or the people in real life? Because Gloria, the character, isn't supposed to like Alexa. If Gloria likes the good doctor, but the good doctor likes Alexa, there would be jealousy involved, or are you talking about the women when they weren't playing a role?" This was becoming rather complicated.

"I don't know. I didn't ask Bandit that," Iggy said.

"Then maybe Bethany—I really need to ask someone what her last name is—should go on our white board list of suspects."

"I agree," Jaxson said.

Rihanna stood and jotted down Bethany's name on the board. "Maybe this Bethany person really liked this actor who played the doctor, and Janet really wanted him for herself. That meant Bethany had the means, motive, and opportunity to do the crime."

My cousin was right. "It will be hard to wait for Levy to get back to us, but I think his information is critical. We need to know how Janet was killed."

A knock sounded on our office door, and Hunter Ashwell, Penny's boyfriend, stuck his head in. He looked like he'd aged ten years.

I jumped up. "What's wrong?"

He rushed in. "It's horrible. Steve just arrested Penny for the murder of Janet Wood."

"What? That can't be true. Sit down and tell me what happened."

Considering his best friend was Nash Solano, the deputy, Hunter would have the inside scoop.

"To be honest, I don't believe Steve really thinks that Penny is capable of killing anyone. He can't, can he? Penny barely knew Janet, yet somehow there is quite a bit of evidence against Penny. I know it's his duty to bring her in, but I still don't like it."

That was ridiculous. "What evidence?"

"You know how Penny's character has to wear that boot every time she goes to the doctor's office?" he asked.

"Yes."

"They found those same boot marks outside of Janet's trailer."

I shook my head. "Penny doesn't take that boot home. She leaves it in the prop room at night."

"I'll tell Steve that, though he'll just say she could have returned it after the murder."

"What does Penny say about what might have happened to Janet?" Rihanna asked.

"She doesn't know, other than she didn't harm the actress. But you know Penny. She's a little freaked out and isn't really thinking straight."

I tapped a finger to my lips as I tried out a few scenarios. "There must be more. Walking in front of the trailer doesn't mean Penny killed anyone, and Steve would realize that."

"That's true, but Penny's fingerprints were on the trailer's outside door handle and on the counter inside of the trailer."

"What about on the inside door handle?"

"He didn't say."

Something wasn't right. "Steve fingerprinted the entire trailer?"

"He must have."

"Does Steve have any other evidence?" Jaxson asked.

"Elissa called and told him that Janet was murdered by a person of magic."

I huffed. "Steve does realize he's the sheriff of Witch's Cove, right? There are a lot of people who are witches and warlocks in this town. Not only that, Bethany, the woman who plays Gloria, is a witch, assuming I can believe Bandit," I threw in.

"Who's Bandit?" Hunter asked.

I explained about Janet's familiar. "He's a trouble maker, but I see no reason for him to lie."

"I know that Penny couldn't hurt a fly. What is Steve thinking arresting her?" Hunter stabbed a hand through his hair.

"Maybe he wants to make the real killer think that he got away with it." Or I hoped that was what Steve was thinking. "Did Nash tell you anything?"

His chuckle came out rueful. "My best friend break confidence? No. And if this is a ploy to get to the real killer, both of them were smart not to tell me. I might not have reacted the same way. I sure hope he lets Penny in on his secret if there is one."

"Me too." I wish there was something more I could tell him. "We're about to list who might have wanted Janet dead. Because of the way she died, I even have Levy on the case. The circumstances of Janet's death are really strange. I'd tell you the details, but you really don't want to know. All I can say is that I don't believe Penny possesses the skill to do what the killer did to Janet." Too bad I wasn't sure what that was exactly.

Hunter blew out a breath. "That's good to hear, but how do we prove it to Steve?"

That was the question. "I don't know. Our best bet is to find more evidence that points to someone else."

Hunter closed his eyes for a moment. "How do we do that?"

I guess that meant he was on board. "I haven't figured that out yet."

"We do have three animals who can help," Jaxson reminded us.

"I don't think Hunter wants to shift into his wolf form and snoop around," I said.

Hunter held up a hand. "I will do whatever I need to do in order to prove Penny isn't guilty."

"Actually, there are more people—or rather enti-ties—who can help. We have Ruby and our two gargoyle shifters. I'm sure Elizabeth and Andorra will help with any spell if need be," Jaxson said.

I smiled. "Then we might solve this case after all. Since Elissa told Steve that magic was involved, our sheriff will have to include us in the case—and by *us*, I mean all of us."

"Hopefully, that's true," Jaxson shot back.

Rihanna leaned forward. "Where did Penny say she was the night Janet was murdered?"

Hunter grunted. "That's the problem. Steve told me that Janet's time of death was between eight and ten at night. While Penny was with Glinda until 8:30 PM, Steve said she could have gone to Janet's trailer, done the deed, and then driven home."

"That is bogus. Penny had to be up at five thirty for her shift. She would have chosen a different night to do the killing, if she'd wanted to do in Janet," I said, becoming angrier by the minute.

"You don't have to convince me," her boyfriend said.

"What about her son?" Rihanna asked.

Hunter shook his head. "Tommy was in the house, but Penny said when she looked in on him, he was asleep. That means, he can't vouch for her whereabouts."

"I'm not sure the courts would take the word of a nine-year-old regarding the time his mom came home anyway," Jaxson tossed out.

"Maybe not," Hunter said.

"There has to be something we can do," I said.

"You tell me. I'll do whatever it takes to prove that Penny didn't do this," he said.

"Maybe Steve will let me speak with her. While we weren't on the set together very often, I did watch her scene with Samuel. If prompted, Penny might think of someone who wanted Janet dead."

"You can try. Steve told me I could visit once. That was it, but maybe you can see her. I'm sure she'd appreciate it."

That was odd. "Since when is Steve a stickler for the rules—especially for us?" Not that I even knew the visiting schedule.

"Glinda," Jaxson said. "Since he needs your help with the magic part, you could insist that you speak with her."

"You are a smart man."

"I try."

"Why don't you take Bandit with you when you speak with Penny?" Rihanna suggested.

That was a terrible idea. "Why?"

"I'm betting Steve will believe that Bandit knows who came and went from that trailer. What if Bandit said that Penny never stepped foot inside the trailer?"

"Her fingerprints were inside," I said. "Besides, who's to say Steve would believe a raccoon, especially one who is a troublemaker?"

"He probably wouldn't." Jaxson scooted closer. "As for finding Penny's fingerprints into the trailer, a smart killer could find a way to lift her prints off of something —like her boot—and then use them to plant evidence."

I whistled. "I wouldn't know how to do that."

"I bet if I look online, I could find out," Jaxson said. "I imagine Steve knows this, too."

"If he does, Steve shouldn't have arrested her." My fiancé could find anything on the Internet. "I'm going to see what Steve has to say."

"Tell Penny how worried I am about her," Hunter said.

"I will."

"What about Bandit?" Iggy said. "Do you want me to find him for you?"

"Sure. While I check in with Steve, how about asking Bandit if he wants to help?"

I left and headed across the street. Part of me hoped Steve wasn't there. I wanted him to be out and about looking for the real killer instead of patting himself on the back for selecting sweet, innocent Penny to pin the rap on.

Once inside the sheriff's office, I instantly smelled my favorite cookies—chocolate chip and spied them a moment later on Pearl's desk.

"Glinda!" Pearl said. Why did she sound so chipper? She had to know why I was there.

"Is Steve here?" I wasn't in the mood for small talk today.

"No, he's out doing sheriff stuff."

"Does that mean he's trying to track down a killer?"

Pearl did the zip-the-lip motion. "Nash is here, though."

"Fine. I'd like to speak with him."

She nodded that I go on back. Nash was at his desk and spun around in his chair as I approached. Being a werewolf like Hunter, his hearing and sense of smell were strong. "Glinda, I'm glad you're here."

Why was that? I would have asked, but I didn't want to go on the defensive right away? "I'd like to see Penny. I'm hoping that since we both were in the movie that she might have a clue as to who really killed the actress."

He lifted his chin. "I'm afraid I can't let you do that."

"Why not?"

"Steve's orders."

That was so lame. "Why would he say that? I've visited other prisoners in their cells." At the moment, I couldn't remember who, but it shouldn't matter. "If Steve wants my help with the case—since magic is involved—he'll agree."

"Sorry."

What? Why was I being stonewalled? "You can search me. I'm not carrying a knife or any kind of weapon."

"Come back tomorrow. Maybe you can see her then." Nash looked rather uncomfortable. No doubt, he was hiding something, or else he felt guilty for denying me the right to visit my friend.

I knew when I was defeated, but this wouldn't be the last he heard from me. "Fine."

As I headed out, I grabbed two cookies. "Thank you, Pearl."

Believe it or not, I wasn't completely discouraged. Just because neither Hunter nor myself could see her, it didn't mean someone with special powers couldn't.

Hello, Genevieve!

CHAPTER FIVE

THERE WAS MORE than one way to skin a cat. I was surprised that neither Steve nor Nash wanted me to speak with Penny, but it didn't mean that others couldn't.

Instead of heading back to the office, I went straight to the Hex and Bones Apothecary. Inside, the owner's two granddaughters, Elizabeth and Andorra, were there. Since Andorra's familiar was Hugo, and Hugo's girlfriend was Genevieve, I needed to speak to Andorra.

"This is a nice surprise," she said.

"I'm afraid it's not a social call. I wish it were."

"Oh, no. What's wrong?"

"Hunter just stopped by the office and told us that Steve arrested Penny for the death of that actress."

"What?"

"I know, right?" I looked around. Two people were within hearing distance. "Can we talk in private?"

While there were a couple of people in the store, I bet her cousin could handle those customers.

Andorra motioned to Elizabeth that she'd be in the back room. When we entered, I was happy to see both Genevieve and Hugo were there having their usual silent discussion. I wish I could communicate telepathically—at least I think I wished that, though there was some gratification in hearing voices.

Genevieve spun around. "Glinda, how nice to see you."

"You, too, but I have a favor to ask you."

She grinned. "Tell me."

Genevieve, our resident gargoyle shifter was always happy to help. "Did you hear about the woman who was murdered the other day? She was a main character in the movie that's being made in town."

"Yes. Janet Wood."

I was impressed she was so up to speed on things. That boded well for her ability to help. I told her about my findings with my magical necklace and also what Elissa said Janet's condition was at the time of death. "I'm sure magic was used to kill her. Have you ever heard of anyone able to do that blood removal thing?"

"No. That's definitely not in my repertoire—or Hugo's for that matter. At least I don't think he can do that." She looked over at him. A moment later she turned back to us. "No. He could harm someone significantly if he wanted to, but he's never had the desire to commit a crime."

"Good to know."

I was sure she could help in another way. "I'm here because Steve arrested Penny."

"No way," she said.

I repeated all of the evidence that Steve had against her, which I still thought was very thin. "Would you mind teleporting into the jail cell and find out what Penny has to say? Steve won't let me see her. I know she'd appreciate some assurance that we are working hard to prove she is innocent."

"No problem. Be back in a sec."

And then she was gone. I had to say, this might have been the first time that she actually warned us that she was taking off. What concerned me was that Genevieve returned in less than a minute.

"What did Penny say?" I asked.

"She's not there. No one was in any of the jail cells in fact."

I turned to Andorra. "I wonder if Steve let her go?"

She shrugged. "That, or her arrest could have been a ruse on his part."

I faced Genevieve. "Can you go to Penny's house and see if she is there?" I gave her the address. "It's a white, one-story house. I'm betting there will be a dark green bike on the lawn. Her son, Tommy, never stores it in the garage where it belongs."

"Sure thing."

Genevieve left. I hope she remembered to knock on the front door instead of just popping up inside. Even though it wasn't Penny's first experience with Genevieve appearing out of nowhere, it might startle her.

"Why do you think Steve told Hunter that he'd arrested Penny if he planned to let her go a few hours later?" Andorra asked.

"Beats me, but some new evidence must have come to light. That or Steve is hoping the real killer will relax and get sloppy."

"Sloppy about what?" she asked. "Do you think this is a person who plans on killing again any time soon?"

I inhaled, my thoughts jumbled. "I don't know, but Steve doesn't do something without a plan."

"If that's the case, why hasn't Penny told Hunter

that she's free? She has to know that he'd be really worried."

I pointed a finger at her. "That is a good question. Hunter or Jaxson would have called if she'd reached out."

Genevieve returned. "Penny's home."

The relief was intense. "That's great. What did she say?"

"She said she's under house arrest, but I'm not so sure that is what's happening. She claimed that since she has to take care of her son, Steve let her go home. Her lack of eye contact made me think she wasn't being totally honest."

I was impressed that Genevieve knew what lack of eye contact meant. "I agree that Penny's excuse is rather flimsy," I said. "Her ex-husband or her mom could have watched Tommy, which means you are right to suspect that something else is going on." I wish I could figure out what it was.

"She said that Steve told her she couldn't talk to anybody." Genevieve smiled. "But I told her I wasn't a person."

That was clever. "What did Penny say to that?"

"She told me I was as much of a person as you or Andorra are."

"See? How could someone that sweet harm anyone?" I asked.

"Penny didn't try to convince you that she didn't kill Janet?" Andorra asked.

"Nope," Genevieve said. The twinkle in her eye implied she was pleased with her command of our slang.

"Penny not telling Genevieve much convinces me this whole thing is a set up—or I hope it is," I said.

"If I'd been accused of murder, I'd tell everyone who would listen that I was innocent," Andorra said.

"Me, too. That's good information, Genevieve. If Penny had been accused of murder for real, she'd have asked you to find me and tell me that she needs our help."

"I agree with you, Glinda," Andorra said. "It explains why she hasn't even called Hunter. I bet that it is killing her to keep that information from him, though"

"Totally. That means I need to tell Hunter that something weird is going on. Then I have to wait for Levy to get back to me. Ugh. This whole case is just bizarre." I wagged a finger. "Steve will pay for this."

Andorra chuckled. "Poor Steve. Let me know if I can help in any way—or if our two special friends can do more." She nodded to Genevieve and Hugo.

"Will do." I held up a finger. "I mentioned that Janet's familiar, Bandit, was hanging around Iggy, right?"

"Yes. What's going to happen to him?" Andorra asked. Then her eyes widened. "Don't even think about asking me to take a second familiar."

I smiled. "No. I can't imagine anyone wanting that trouble maker. I'm hoping that Janet has a family member who would be willing to be his new host."

"Do you know this person's name so you can ask him or her?" Andorra asked.

"No, but I'll ask the director or Samuel Lipstein. Someone in the cast must know. Thanks for helping."

"I didn't do anything," Andorra said.

"Being a sounding board is a big help." I hugged her goodbye and left. Hunter would be even more anxious by now. As much as I wanted to talk with Penny, I believed Hunter could get the truth out of her the quickest. My bestie could only hold out for so long. That much I was certain.

I rushed up the office steps and entered, hoping Hunter was still there. He was.

Penny's boyfriend jumped up. "What did she say? Did Steve let you see her?"

"Nothing and no." I sat next to Rihanna and explained that Steve wasn't there and that Nash wouldn't let me go back either.

"That's what happened to me."

"That's because Penny wasn't in the jail."

"What? What do you mean?" Hunter asked.

I told them about using Genevieve to get to the bottom of this. "Penny is home, but she's claiming she is under house arrest and can't contact or speak with anyone. Personally, I'm not buying it."

Hunter stood. "I don't either. I'll convince her to speak with me."

Good. "Let us know."

He nodded, and as soon as he rushed out, I turned to the others. "Any ideas why Steve is doing this?"

"I wish I did," Jaxson said.

Iggy crawled toward the door. "Where are you going?" I asked him.

"We need Bandit. He and I need to snoop."

As much as I wasn't sure about Janet's familiar, I believed he could help. "Can you ask him to come here for a bit first? I'm thinking he knows more than he realizes."

"Really?"

Why did he sound so surprised—and so happy? True, I hadn't exactly been warm toward his new friend, but that was because I thought he was a bad influence on Iggy. "Yes, really."

"Okay, I'll be back soon if I can find him. He was MIA before." He jetted through the cat door.

While Iggy could scurry pretty fast when he wanted to, his long distance traveling wasn't exactly speedy. If he didn't know where Bandit was located, it could take him a while to find his friend.

"Glinda, can you make a list of all of the people in the movie?" Rihanna asked.

"Sure, but I don't know everyone's real name."

Jaxson held up a finger. "I thought you were going to find out."

"I was, but then I became distracted."

"That's okay. We can do this another way. What is the name of the actor who plays the doctor?" he asked.

"Samuel Lipstein."

"Got it." Jaxson moved over his computer and typed in that name. He scrolled down. "Found it."

Rihanna and I went over to his desk. "What does it say?"

"It gives the cast list for *No Love Potion Needed,* but it's dated six months ago."

"I bet things have changed. I know Penny and I aren't on the original list since we are just extras, but there might be other new hires."

"Agreed, but I can start cross referencing all of these names on the cast list. I bet some have worked with Janet before. There might be some bad blood that we don't know about."

I leaned back in my chair. "You are a talented man."

He grinned. "That's why I'm with you."

My heart sang. He was the best. "Rihanna, let's fire up that white board."

"You got it."

We moved over to the sofa area. Rihanna handed the board to me, and I placed it on my lap. She then sat next to me. "I don't know where to begin." That was unusual for me.

"You said the character Gloria kills Alexa in the book, right?" she asked.

"Yes. I'll put her down, but why would Bethany harm Janet? Unless, she was actually falling for Samuel Lipstein, and he only has eyes for Janet. Then Bethany might have a reason to want Janet dead." Because that was the best I could come up with, I wrote her name down. "I'll put jealousy for the motive. I can't even guess a ranking for her likelihood for murder."

"Leave it blank for now. Who's next?"

"Samuel Lipstein, but what would be his motive for killing Janet?"

"Maybe Janet was obsessed with him. She might have been spreading lies about him, saying that the actor cared for her, when in reality, he liked someone else," Rihanna said.

I chuckled. "You might have missed your calling."

"What's that?"

"You should write romance novels."

"That isn't going to happen. It would drive me crazy to write about misunderstandings when a simple discussion could solve everything." Rihanna nodded to the board. "Put down Samuel Lipstein. He might not have liked Janet for some other reason."

I scribbled down his name. "Lynn Lurch should be next," I said. "While she is super sweet, she was Janet's understudy. It's possible that she really wanted the role badly."

"We're grasping at straws, aren't we?" Rihanna asked.

"Yes, but we need to start somewhere. The problem is that there aren't that many people in the movie."

Rihanna shrugged. "It could be a crew member or a member of the staff."

"True."

"What about the director, or should we call him the producer?" Rihanna asked.

"Either name works since Shawn acts as both. I can attest to the fact that he didn't seem to like Janet," I said. "She would often forget her lines, and she wasn't always on time. That upset him quite a lot." I wrote down Shawn Shields.

"You said the screenwriter found the body, right?" she asked.

"Yes, but I don't see where he fits in. However, for the sake of completeness, I'll list Chris Pena. He had shown some disgust at Janet when she didn't interpret her lines like he'd written them."

Rihanna scrunched up her face. "That's the director's job, not the screenwriter's."

"Tell me about it." This was getting worse by the minute. "There is a diner owner, but I don't think she's had her scene yet."

I had listed Bethany from before. When I read over the board, it was clear we had little to go on. Just then Iggy came in the cat door, followed by Bandit. The raccoon stopped as soon as he was inside and looked around.

"Hi, Bandit." I wanted to sound friendly. This animal might be the key to this case.

The raccoon looked over at Iggy. "Can they really understand me?"

Iggy faced me, obviously expecting me to answer. When I said nothing, he answered for me. "Yes, she can. You can move closer. No one bites. Janet's death has been such a shock to all of us, and we want to help."

Sheesh. That might have been true, but he sounded like he'd listened to my father—the funeral director—one too many times.

Bandit inched closer, and Iggy stayed right by his side.

"Iggy said you wanted to know about Janet, my host."

"Yes. Did you see anything the night she died?" I asked.

"Maybe."

Bandit was cautious, and I could appreciate that. "I'm quite certain that magic was used to kill her. Can you help in any way?" I asked.

CHAPTER SIX

"Like I told Iggy, Janet had a lot of people coming and going into the trailer. When anyone visited, she had me hide in the bedroom. Since I can cloak myself, I sometimes spied on them." Bandit stuck out his chest. Someone must have taught him what that meant.

"I am sorry that happened to you, but I'm glad you weren't left out completely." I wasn't sure what else I should say.

"That's true, but I'll tell you one thing. I'm not as lucky as Iggy is. He has the perfect life." He glanced over at my familiar, but I couldn't read his expression.

I have to say that I hadn't expected Iggy to portray his life as being cushy, even though it was. "He does have it good."

"I bet you never send him to his room, do you?" Bandit asked.

That might be because Iggy slept in the living room. I was the one who went to my room. "No. Would you like to come over to the sofa area so we chat more comfortably?"

Bandit looked over at Iggy. "Okay."

He loped over while Iggy crawled. I expected both of them to climb onto the furniture, but they remained on the floor, next to the coffee table.

"Who visited Janet the most?" I asked Bandit.

"That Samuel guy."

"Did he come over to rehearse lines?"

Bandit looked over at Iggy. "I don't want to say in front of the kid."

I had to work not to laugh. "Iggy is sixteen."

"As I said, he's a kid."

"I think Iggy is old enough to hear what you have to say." I'm not sure what Bandit was so reluctant to tell us.

"Fine. They were kissing and *stuff*."

I didn't need the details then. "So that I am clear, you're saying that even outside of the movie set, Samuel Lipstein and Janet liked each other?"

"You met her," he said.

The raccoon sounded rather sarcastic, so I assumed it meant Samuel didn't really care for Janet.

Personally, I never liked her. She was arrogant and entitled, but her familiar might have really cared for her. At least, I hope he had.

"Many times. Are you saying that the actor was only pretending to like her for some reason? And by that, I mean he actually didn't like her as much as he was supposed to on the set?" Though why would he be kissing her and *stuff*? Unless he needed something from her.

Bandit placed a paw on his forehead. "You don't get it. I'm pretty sure Samuel didn't like Janet. Heck, I didn't even like her much, but I was kind of stuck with her since I'm not a total animal, you know."

Wow. That was sad about him not liking his host. Bandit enjoyed the comforts of the human world, however. I could see that. "If Samuel didn't like her, were they just practicing some *scene?*"

Bandit turned to Iggy. "I thought you said Glinda was smart."

Ouch.

"She is," Iggy said. "Sometimes."

Bandit dipped his head for a moment. "Didn't Iggy tell you that Janet set her sights on Samuel— only he wasn't interested in her? Alexa, the character, was supposed to do a love spell on Sam, the actor, so that he would fall in love with her, much to the dismay of Gloria."

"And Gloria kills Alexa later on in the show. Yes, I had heard that was the movie plot."

Bandit held up a hand, acting way too human-like. It was almost creepy, even though I was used to our two gargoyle shifters, Genevieve and Hugo, acting like they were completely human.

"Yes, but did you know that Janet did a *real* love spell on Samuel?" I swear Bandit wiggled his eyebrows.

I had conducted quite a few spells, but I wasn't aware a spell could make someone fall in love. "No, I did not."

"A love spell really exists?" Rihanna asked. "That is so cool."

"No, a love spell is not cool," I shot back. "Two people need to fall in love naturally. Spells wear off, you know."

"Not all spells wear off," Bandit said, lifting his head. "Though this one kind of did."

Was he a bonafide warlock now? I turned to Jaxson and Rihanna. "If Bandit's information is correct, this gives us motivation for Samuel and Bethany to want Janet dead." Was it possible that Janet's death was a joint venture between these two? Bethany was a witch.

"I can see Samuel wanting Janet dead if he found out that she'd tricked him into falling in love with her," Rihanna said. "The spell might only work some of the time, not that I even know if that is possible."

Jaxson nodded. "I agree, but not about Bethany wanting to do in Janet, unless Bethany really cared for Samuel."

I turned my focus back to our informant. "Bandit, besides Bethany and Samuel, who else didn't like Janet?"

"Didn't like, or hated her enough to kill her?" he asked.

He had a point. "Hated her enough to kill her."

"I don't know."

"No one comes to mind?" I asked.

"Nope."

He wasn't any help.

"What else can you tell us about Janet's experience in Witch's Cove," Jaxson asked. "Was she upset about anything?"

He scratched his head, which seemed a bit dramatic. "She didn't like that screenwriter guy, Chris something, but I couldn't stand him either."

"Why was that?" I asked. Bandit didn't seem to like anyone—except maybe Iggy.

"He thought everyone should do what he wanted. He interpreted the novel and wrote the screenplay, and because of that, the actors needed to listen to *him*—not the director."

That wasn't good. I wonder why the director didn't ask Chris to go home. Or was there something between them?

Before I could voice my opinion, the office door blew open and a smiling Hunter and Penny rushed in. I jumped up, ran over to her, and hugged her. "You're free?"

"Yes. It was crazy. Okay, the whole thing was a plot to catch the real killer," Penny said.

I knew it. "Come sit down. I want to hear all about it. Penny, you know Bandit." I introduced the raccoon to Hunter, but I told him that Hunter wouldn't be able to understand him.

"Just great. Do you have any idea how frustrating my life has been not being understood?" Bandit was obviously looking for sympathy.

"I'm sure it's been terrible, but before we hear your life story, I need to know why our sheriff arrested Penny for your host's murder."

He climbed onto the coffee table. Apparently, he was interested too. "Fine. She can talk."

How generous of him. I looked over at Penny. "Tell us!"

"Steve has a few suspects only he wouldn't tell me who they are. Here was the deal. He actually *paid* me to stay at home for two to three days. Turns out the trap worked." Penny grinned.

My mind was blown. This wasn't Steve's normal method of solving a crime. "What trap?"

"We all know that Hugo and Genevieve love to help solve crimes," she said. "Right?"

"Most definitely." My mouth dropped. "Don't tell me Steve asked for their help?"

Iggy perked up. "What? And Hugo didn't tell me?"

I turned toward him. "Tell me, young man, when was the last time you actually visited your friend?" I didn't want to remind him of the company he'd been keeping of late.

"Oh, yeah, there's that. I wish we had a way of communicating long distance."

"That would be nice," I said, "but I don't think either of you can use a cell phone effectively." Besides, Hugo was mute.

Iggy stuck his tongue out at me. We'd have to have a talk later about his defiance. I faced Penny again. "What did our friends do for Steve?"

"They were sentries. I don't know the details, but since they can be invisible and don't need to eat or sleep, one of them stayed in Janet's trailer and the other one remained outside. If anyone tried to get into the trailer for any reason, Genevieve would go to Steve and tell him."

"I trust someone showed up?" Jaxson asked.

"Yes. Samuel did," she said.

I hadn't expected her to say his name. "Was he looking for something?"

"He said he was looking for evidence against our producer/director. He believes that Shawn killed Janet," Penny said.

"I hadn't suspected Shawn, but that's great. Do we know why Shawn would kill Janet?"

"Not yet," Penny said.

"What I want to know is why didn't Genevieve tell me she was aware of this whole arrest-Penny hoax?" I asked.

"Steve told her not to say anything, and that if you asked her to check up on me, she couldn't tell you or anyone else about it being a set up. If she did, he couldn't ever trust her again."

My mouth opened. "That sneaky gargoyle shifter. Or rather that sneaky sheriff."

"I admire her for that," Jaxson said. "That had to have been very hard for her to keep a secret like that."

"That's true, but I'd like to hear what Genevieve has to say. I'd also like to know what Steve is doing with this information."

"All I know is that he took Shawn in for questioning—after he spoke with Samuel, of course," Penny said.

I turned to Bandit. "Do you have any reason to believe that Shawn Shields is a warlock?"

"No."

"No, you don't think he is one, or you know for a fact he isn't one?"

"Janet said he wasn't one."

That was a reputable source. "If that is true, I'm betting Shawn didn't kill her then. The hard part will be proving to Steve that Shawn doesn't have any magical powers."

"I can do my trick and shout at him to see if he answers," Iggy said.

"I know you can do that, but let's first see if we need to go that route."

"I tried talking to him once or twice," Bandit said, "but he didn't answer, though you didn't answer either. Why was that?"

"It's simple. I didn't know who you would tell. I also don't know these people in the movie very well, and I wasn't comfortable having them know I am a witch," I said.

"Janet let people know she was one," Bandit said.

That was Janet, all right. She seemed like the type to want to be the center of attention. "Since she is playing a witch in the movie, that would be a natural thing to tell people, but I doubt a lot of folks believed her."

"Yeah. She might have mentioned that."

I looked over at Penny. "Something has been bothering me. Hunter told us that Steve found your fingerprints inside of Janet's trailer. Were you ever inside?"

She smiled. "No. Steve made that up. He needed to have people believe that I was a viable suspect."

My admiration for our sheriff shot up. "That was good thinking."

"What are you going to do now, Glinda?" Jaxson asked. "I know you'll want to see what Steve is up to, but do you really think he'll tell you anything?"

That was always the issue. "No, but I bet someone I know can find out."

"Hugo?" Iggy asked.

I was going to ask Genevieve, but Hugo might never have agreed to remain silent—mostly because he couldn't talk—but that didn't mean he couldn't tell Iggy or Andorra what he learned. "Precisely, but I'm hoping Jaxson can do a deep dive into Shawn Shields first. Samuel Lipstein must have had an idea what to look for in Janet's trailer."

"I can do that." Jaxson returned to his computer. "Any idea what I should be searching for?"

"No, but Samuel must have found something in Janet's trailer that was enough for Steve to bring Shawn in," I said.

"Are you thinking blackmail?" Rihanna asked.

Bandit spun around to face me. "Oh, wait a minute. I remember something."

"What is it?" I asked.

"I don't know the details, but Janet mentioned that Shawn cheated, and she found out about it. She said she'd tell if he didn't give her a big role in this movie."

This was huge! "Cheated how?" I asked.

"I can't remember. You should ask the *doctor*." Bandit slightly shook his head. "Though that man couldn't put a Band-Aid on a cut."

I wonder if he picked up his sarcastic tendencies from his host. "His doctoring skills might be lacking since Samuel is an actor, but if he found evidence that pointed to Shawn as the killer, he can't be all that dumb."

Bandit dropped down onto his stomach. "I bet Janet told him what Shawn had done."

"You don't have any idea what this cheating was referring to?" I asked. "I can't imagine she'd care if her director was having an affair. I don't think he's even married." Of course, I could be wrong, though I was leaning more toward him being with Chris Pena. He could have cheated on Chris, however.

"No. Not that kind of cheating."

Bandit wasn't very good at spilling the beans.

"What other kind of cheating are you talking about? Did he cheat on his taxes or something?"

"I may have something," Jaxson said.

I turned to him. "What did you find?"

"It may not be anything, but Shawn Shields won a prestigious movie award, which was why the movie studio gave him money to direct and produce *No Love Potion Needed*."

I couldn't figure out why that was important. "That's great, but what's wrong with that?"

"Apparently, the movie he entered wasn't his own."

CHAPTER SEVEN

"WHAT DO you mean the movie Shawn entered into the contest wasn't his own?" I asked.

"I don't think there is much to the rumor, because he received funding from the studio," Jaxson said. "However, the article claims that a Benson McDaniels created some movie short, and that Shawn stole it and entered it into the contest as his own."

I whistled. "I'm assuming the people who bestowed the award didn't believe this Benson McDaniels was the creator?"

"Apparently not," Jaxson said.

"How can we find out if there is any truth to McDaniels' claim?" Penny asked.

Jaxson turned back to the computer. "Let me see what I can find out."

"Penny, Steve didn't give you any hint that he thought Shawn might be guilty, did he?" I asked.

"No. All I know was that I would be having two to three paid vacation days, and I was okay with that." She turned to Hunter and clasped his hand. "The worst part was knowing that Hunter would be upset thinking I was still in jail."

He leaned over and planted a kiss on her. "You're good now, and that's all that matters."

Penny's stomach grumbled. "Though a meal is in order."

"Then let's get thee to a diner!" Hunter said with a grin.

They both stood and said their goodbyes. "Let me know if you learn anything," Penny said.

"Will do."

Once they left, I turned back to Bandit. "Now that Janet has passed, is there someone you can stay with? Like a relative of hers?"

He looked over at Iggy. The slight lift of my familiar's leg implied Iggy had been hoping I'd let Bandit stay with us.

"Janet has a sister who lives across the state," he told her.

That was hopeful. "Do you know her name?"

"Valerie Upton."

"Do you think she'd be willing to take you in?" I asked.

He seemed to glare at me. "I don't know."

"You don't happen to know her phone number or anything, do you?"

"Do I look like a rolodex?"

I almost snorted. I'm surprised he knew what one of those things was. I'd personally never used one since it was before my time. "I bet Steve has Janet's phone, and Valerie's contact information should be listed. This is a good thing since it will give me an excuse to speak with him."

Jaxson smiled. "What you really want is the information on what he has on the director, right?"

I shrugged and then smiled. "Your point being?"

"Head on over then, though I'm not sure you'll learn as much as you'd like."

I thought about asking Iggy to come with me, but if Steve refused to deliver the needed intel, I might have a better chance of collecting it if one of the gargoyle shifters helped. "Be back in a flash."

As soon as I stepped outside, I realized I should have grabbed a sweater, but I didn't want to take the time to go back for one. Being high season, cars were streaming down the street, forcing me to use the button at the crosswalk. Once it turned green, I hustled across and strode to the sheriff's department.

Inside, both Pearl and Jennifer Larson were there in the middle of changing shifts. Darn. I had better luck learning things from Pearl. Jen was rather tight-lipped.

Pearl looked up. "Hi, Glinda. Penny isn't here. Steve released her."

Either she thought I didn't know, or she wanted Jen to hear that she hadn't spilled the beans. "Actually, I just saw her. I'm here, because I'm trying to track down a relative of Janet's. I thought Steve might know."

"He's busy with another suspect."

I imagined she was referring to Shawn Shields.

Jennifer placed a hand on Pearl's arm. "I'll try to help Glinda. You go on home."

Pearl winced, clearly recognizing a brush off when she heard it. "Sure."

"Why do you need to track down Janet's relation?" Jen asked me.

"I need to find a forever home for Janet's raccoon."

"Why not take him to an animal shelter?"

Apparently, she had no idea that Bandit was a familiar. "Bandit is like Iggy. He can talk to those who can hear him."

"Oh. I didn't know. Let me see what I can find out. Stay here."

Suddenly, I felt like a *persona non grata*. If Steve was interrogating a potential killer, I understood why I couldn't interrupt, but Jen acted as if I was the criminal. I wonder what I did to warrant that response?

Jen disappeared down the hallway, hopefully to have a word with Steve. I was happy she hadn't told me to return tomorrow.

A few minutes later, Jen returned with a piece of paper in her hand. "This is the sister's contact information. Her name is Valerie Upton."

"Thanks." I nodded toward where Steve's office was located. "I heard he thinks our director killed Janet?"

"I wouldn't know."

Of course, she did. Jen just wouldn't say. "Thanks for the contact information."

As soon as I left, I hung a right and went straight to the Hex and Bones. I really wanted to know what Steve was asking Shawn. If Steve arrested him, that might be the end of the movie unless they could find another director. Someone was going to lose a lot of money if they couldn't.

Inside the store, I found Elizabeth manning the checkout counter and Bertha over by the pile of spell books talking with a customer. I didn't see Andorra, though.

I went up to Elizabeth. "Hey. Is Genevieve or Hugo around?"

"No, they are doing something with Andorra. I don't know what, though. Is something wrong?"

"Did Andorra tell you about Penny's arrest?"

"She did, but I still can't believe it."

"That's because it was a ruse." I explained Steve's plan. "Apparently, the ruse worked since he snagged Shawn Shields, the producer/director, as the possible killer."

"I didn't know him. How can I help?" Elizabeth asked.

"I was really hoping to find out what is going on in that interrogation that is happening as we speak."

She smiled. "And you thought you could send one of our special friends to check it out."

"Something like that."

Just then Ruby came around from behind the counter. "What about me?" the cat asked.

Elizabeth had recently agreed to be Ruby's host after her original host had passed away. Ruby was a very special cat in that she had the ability to enhance other familiars' abilities. She also could teleport and cloak herself, but both of those talents were a bit inconsistent. However, desperate times called for desperate measures. "Did you hear me tell Elizabeth what was happening?"

"Yes! You need someone to spy for you."

She always did cut to the chase. I hoped she and Bandit never got together. The two of them would spell disaster. "I do. I want to know why our sheriff thinks that the movie director might have killed Janet."

"Got it. Be right back." Just like Genevieve, Ruby disappeared.

"I'm not sure I like Ruby doing this," Elizabeth said.

"If she happens to appear by mistake, Steve will figure out what's up. Though in case her cloaking doesn't work, I'm hoping Ruby will crawl under a chair or hide in the corner." Elizabeth's lips pressed together. "You know I wouldn't ask if it wasn't important."

"I know. It's not like Ruby is going into a den of criminals."

"True. I'm going to head back to the office. Can you ask Ruby to stop over afterward?" She could teleport, and she knew where our office was located.

"I sure can."

I left, but my anxiety level didn't return to normal. What if the director was the murderer, and Steve didn't have enough evidence against him to hold him? Our sheriff would have to let him go. If that happened, I'd probably feel a bit strange going back to the set when Shawn was barking orders at us.

I crossed the street, hoping that Jaxson had dredged up more information on the man. At least I had the contact information for Janet's sister. Fingers crossed that Valerie would take Bandit. If she agreed, either I'd ask Genevieve to teleport our raccoon familiar across the state, or Jaxson and I would make a road trip out of it.

I trudged up the stairs and went inside the office. Rihanna was looking through some photos on her camera, and Jaxson was at the computer. I didn't know where the animals were. Hopefully, they were staying out of trouble.

Jaxson turned around. "What did Steve say?"

"I wasn't able to speak with him. He was busy grilling our director."

I explained about asking Ruby to listen in on the conversation.

"Smart. Did you find out any information about Janet's sister?" Jaxson asked.

I pulled out the paper from my pocket. "I did. I'm going to call her now to see if she'd be willing to take Bandit."

I sat on the couch next to Rihanna and called Valerie. Since Bandit didn't seem overjoyed to be with her, a trickle of guilt surfaced.

"Hello?" the woman on the other end responded.

I hoped that the sheriff had contacted Valerie about her sister's death. Telling someone their relative had passed would be a total nightmare. So what if my parents owned a funeral home?

"Yes, this is Glinda Goodall, an acquaintance of your sister. I want to say I am sorry for your loss."

"Thank you. Can I help you?"

Wow. That comment came out quite cold. I explained about Bandit and his need for a new home. Considering Janet was a witch, I assumed Valerie was too. "Do you think you could give him a forever home?"

She didn't say anything for a bit. "I don't know. He's quite a handful."

I figured she'd say that. "I think he was just acting out."

She huffed. "I know my sister didn't always pay attention to him like she should have, but raccoons by nature are super curious. They are born to get into trouble."

"That's true, but we're desperate. Is there any way you can take him?"

She huffed out a breath. "I guess I could give him a trial run, but I'm going out of town for a few days. I will call you when I'm free so we can make the exchange."

I had no problem watching over Bandit for a short time. "No problem. I'll watch him. Thank you."

I gave her my contact information and then hung up. Guilt assaulted me once more. I wondered if Bandit might be better off in the wild than with Valerie. She might ignore him more than Janet.

"She said yes?" Jaxson asked.

"She did, but we have to babysit him for a few days since she'll be out of town."

"Cool," Rihanna said. "I like Bandit. He seems like a troubled soul. Kind of like I used to be."

I smiled. "You have come a long way."

"Thank you."

My cell rang, and I thought it might be Valerie telling me she'd made a mistake. When I checked the caller ID. I found it was Levy. Yes! "Hey there. Any luck finding what might have killed Janet?"

"I'm sad to say no. I asked around, though. I can't say how it works, but there was a warlock who could kill someone by placing his hands near the person's head. No one knows for sure what he did to them, except that it stopped brain activity. I didn't find out anything about this blood loss stuff. Either way, the person died."

"At least I know that a person of magic possibly killed Janet. Thank you for your help."

"I wish I could have done more."

"No, that was helpful." I disconnected and told them what Levy said.

"That doesn't tell us a whole lot," Jaxson said. "Does it?"

"Not too much. Steve will believe Levy if he said magic killed Janet." I stood. "I need a tea."

Just as I returned with my glass, Ruby appeared in the office. "Hi!" She sounds happy for a change. "Where's Iggy?"

"I'm not sure." Telling her he had a new best friend might not put her in the greatest of moods, though I wasn't sure how much she liked Iggy. Ruby always wanted to be top dog—or rather the top famil- iar. "Did you learn anything from the sheriff's interview?"

"I learned a lot. Got any meat?"

I chuckled. When she was here the first time, I'd purchased some canned tuna for her just in case she came back. "I'll fix you something, but then you need to reveal the wonders of what was said."

"Sure."

After I fixed her a bowl, I returned with her meal and placed it on the coffee table. Ruby went to town. If I didn't know Elizabeth, I'd think she didn't feed her. Teleporting and staying cloaked probably used a lot of energy though.

Ruby finished, licked her lips, and stretched out.

When she glanced up at me, it was a clear sign that she expected me to remove her bowl, which I did.

"Okay, the sheriff interviewed this Shawn Shields person, but I didn't arrive until after the sheriff was halfway through his questions."

"That's okay. Anything you found out would be helpful."

"I think Janet or Alexa or whatever her name was, might have been blackmailing Mr. Shields."

"Rihanna, you were right. Blackmail was involved." To be fair, that was what Bandit had implied.

My cousin smiled. "Well, well, what do you know? Ruby, do you know what dirt Janet had on the director?"

We all believed we knew that it was about the stolen movie, but it never hurt to get confirmation.

"The director stole someone's movie short, or maybe he said short story. I can't remember. Anyway, he passed if off as his own at some competition. I wasn't there to find out how Janet found out about it, but she made the director give her a major role in this movie in return for not telling the studio," Ruby said.

Once more, Bandit's theory was confirmed. "Blackmail is a good motive for murder," I said. "Did you sense that Steve believed that the killer is a warlock or a witch?"

"He didn't bring it up. Anyway, the director admitted to stealing the guy's work in order to get funding for his movie. But...before you celebrate that the murderer has been arrested, he said he didn't kill the lady. He was with someone named Chris all night."

"Hmm. Chris is the screenwriter. Did Steve say he'd check his alibi?"

"Yes."

I waited for her to say more. "Did the sheriff arrest the director?"

"No."

I looked over at Jaxson. "What do you think?"

"Blackmail alone doesn't mean he murdered Janet. Steve would need physical evidence."

Darn. "I bet Chris confirms that the two of them were together going over the next day's scene. Maybe they were or maybe they weren't. If Chris lied, it might be because he was busy killing Janet."

"Anything is possible, but let's see what Steve does next," Jaxson said.

"I hate waiting." I turned to Ruby. "Thank you for your help. Please thank Elizabeth for us."

"Sure thing. Say hi to Iggy for me."

Maybe there was more to their relationship than I thought.

CHAPTER EIGHT

I LEANED back against the sofa. "What should we do now?" I asked Rihanna and Jaxson.

"If the director is innocent, he might be more cooperative in helping us find the killer," Jaxson said. "However, if Steve doesn't arrest Shawn Shields, it doesn't mean our sheriff won't do so in the near future."

I shivered. "I can't imagine having that hang over my head. That has me curious as to whether Shawn wants to continue with the movie—assuming he is innocent."

"I imagine that would be up to the studio who is backing him," Jaxson said.

"True."

The cat door flap opened and our two trouble

makers waltzed in. "I hope you don't mind if Bandit stays with us for a bit," Iggy said. "He's lonely."

I think Bandit just might be looking for a partner in crime. "Sure. Have a seat. We have news."

Not that either of them actually sat, but Iggy knew what that meant. "What did we miss?" Iggy asked.

For the moment, I thought it best if I didn't say where I received confirmation about the blackmail scheme. My familiar might be upset that I asked Ruby to investigate instead of him. "Steve brought the director in for questioning," I said.

"We saw that," Bandit said.

Oh, really? "When?"

"Iggy and I were hanging out when we spotted the guy being escorted into the sheriff's office. I told you Janet had something on Shawn Shields. I think he killed her, or else he paid someone to kill her."

That was a horrible thought. If this was a murder for hire, we'd never be able to catch the killer—unless the murderer was caught on camera somehow. I hoped what Bandit said was just a guess.

My stomach grumbled. I'd been so busy today that I hadn't eaten much at all. "Anyone up for a diner meal?"

"Sure," Jaxson and Rihanna said in unison.

"What about us?" Bandit asked.

He actually sounded a bit upset. "I'll bring you two a doggie bag or rather a raccoon and lizard bag."

"But you didn't tell us your news." Bandit's tone sounded like a whine.

"I did, but you already knew about the arrest. I'm not sure why Shawn was arrested or what happened in the meeting, but I'll ask around," I said.

"Fine." Bandit headed toward the door. "Come on, Iggy. We need to investigate. I don't think the sheriff is up for the job."

"Where are you two going?" I didn't want Iggy doing anything dangerous. Bottom line was that I didn't trust Bandit.

"Iggy wants to introduce me to Hugo. I think together, we can find more clues."

He might have a point. "Good luck."

Bandit looked over at Iggy. "Hop on my back. We can travel faster that way."

When Iggy looked at me, I couldn't quite tell what he was thinking, but I bet he'd be thumbing his nose at me if he could. As soon as they left, we headed out to eat.

"Do you think Dolly will know anything?" Jaxson asked.

"If Pearl knows, then Dolly will know." So what if Steve's grandmother had gone home already for the day. The woman had a way of finding things out.

"Great."

After entering the diner, I looked to see if Hunter and Penny were still there, but they weren't. Luckily, we snagged the last free remaining booth. No sooner had we settled in than Dolly came over. "Did you hear?"

"Hear what?" There was a lot of information that I'd found out about.

"That good looking Samuel Lipstein confessed to killing Janet Wood."

My mouth dropped open. "There has to be a mistake. Are you sure?"

"Pearl said that according to Steve, once the director left the sheriff's office—I assume you heard about that—that Samuel waltzed in and said he wanted to confess."

We all sat up straighter at the same time. "He actually confessed to killing Janet Wood?"

"He did."

"Why would anyone confess to something like that?" Rihanna asked.

"I have no idea. Pearl said that Jen told her the man was acting really strange when he came in, but she figured if she had walked into the sheriff's office to confess that kind of crime, she would have acted strangely too."

Since my witch radar was telling me that something wasn't right in Kansas, I had a million questions. "Did she say anything else? Like why he killed Janet? Or how?" The last part would be the most important.

"No, just that Steve was interviewing him now."

"Thanks. I'll see what I can find out."

"Great. Be sure to tell me." I nodded. "What can I get you three?"

We all ordered our usual meal. Once she left, I turned to my cohorts. "Why would Samuel turn himself in?"

"I have no idea," Jaxson said.

"Do you think I should find Ruby, Hugo, or Genevieve again, and ask them to snoop?"

"Steve might have asked Genevieve and Hugo to keep quiet about things until the case is solved. It might be safer if you ask Ruby again, but you know it tires her out to cloak herself," Jaxson said.

"You're right. I imagine the details of his confession will be known fairly soon—assuming Pearl can drag the information out of her grandson," I said.

"If Samuel Lipstein is in jail, that leaves both of the leads gone," Jaxson said.

"Glinda, didn't you say that it was Samuel's name that would draw people to the movie?" Rihanna asked.

"Yes, but I imagine Shawn will try to recruit

someone since he's spent weeks on the movie already. He'll probably try to find a replacement equally as famous as Samuel Lipstein," I said.

"That won't be easy," he said. "I say we have a nice meal and then regroup. We can go to the Hex and Bones afterward if you want to see if anyone there knows anything—or can find out."

I smiled. "You have a deal."

During our meal, I considered the pros and cons of using Ruby again to spy on the interview between Steven and Samuel, but eventually I decided to wait until tomorrow. By then, we should know the details of what went down.

Since it was late, we'd normally all head back to our respective homes, but I needed to deliver the food to Iggy and Bandit.

As expected, they were anxious for their meal. I placed the two To-Go boxes on the coffee table and opened the lids. "Enjoy, boys."

They didn't waste any time chowing down. That implied Bandit hadn't broken into any garbage cans lately. I sat on the sofa and waited until they'd finished. "Bandit, I heard that Samuel confessed to killing your host."

He shook his head. "I didn't know that , but he didn't do it."

"How can you be so sure?"

"He isn't a warlock." His matter of fact statement implied he was confident in his assessment.

"Did you hear his confession while you were out and about?"

Bandit looked over at Iggy. "Maybe."

Rihanna sat next to me. "Spill, boys. We're here to help, you know."

Bandit glanced at Iggy again. Iggy nodded, but I highly doubted they could communicate telepathically. "Maybe I saw an opportunity and took it," Bandit said.

"What does that mean?" I asked.

"With Iggy on my back, I cloaked myself and followed Samuel inside. Being curious, I joined their conversation in the sheriff's office."

"You spied on them?" I actually wanted to cheer, but Bandit shouldn't be doing that on his own. What if he'd been caught? I didn't want Steve to be upset at Iggy.

"Spying is a harsh word. We merely listened without their knowledge."

That was the definition of spying. "Fine. What did you learn?"

"I told you she'd want to know," Iggy said.

"Did you suggest this?" I asked my familiar.

"Does it matter?" The head lift meant he had.

"Fine. You joined the interrogation. What

happened?"

"I'll tell her," Iggy said. "Bandit, you're too long-winded."

Iggy possessed a lot of my traits. "Thank you. Go on."

"Let me say that I think the guy was on drugs or something since he kind of sounded like a robot."

Jaxson, who was sitting in the chair across from the sofa, leaned forward. "What do you mean?" Jaxson asked.

"He spoke in kind of the same tone for each word."

"You mean in a monotone?"

"I guess."

That matched what Jennifer Larson told Pearl.

"Did he say why he killed Janet?" I asked.

"He said it was because she'd put a love spell on him. All was good for a while until it wore off. Then he became angry."

"I'd be angry too," I said. "But enough to kill?"

"I'm just telling you what he said," Iggy replied.

"How did he say he killed her?" This would be the key to whether he was guilty or not.

"He said he placed his hands on her head, and then she died."

That matched what Levy had found out. I faced

Bandit. "You're positive that Samuel Lipstein is not a warlock, right?"

"I guess he could have been faking it, but he told Janet he wasn't comfortable being with a witch."

I looked over at Jaxson. "I honestly thought that Bethany and Samuel were a thing."

"In the movie maybe," he said. "We have no idea about real life."

"Good point."

"Don't you think Steve will check out his story?" Rihanna asked.

"How? Samuel Lipstein's motive seems legit. It's his method of death that I'm questioning," I said.

"I bet Steve asks you and Elissa to decide if what Samuel said could have happened."

Rihanna always was very logical. "I guess I'll find out tomorrow."

We discussed a few more points of interest and then called it quits for the evening. "Come on, Iggy. Time to go home."

"What about Bandit?"

"He can stay with us." It wouldn't be fair to Rihanna to have her be responsible for him. "Bandit, if you do stay at my place, under no circumstance are you to go down to the restaurant."

"You live above a restaurant?" I didn't like the excitement in his voice.

"I do."

He shook his head. "How about I stay here then? I don't have that kind of willpower."

I was impressed he understood himself so well. "It's up to Rihanna."

"They can both stay here. Iggy can be in charge of making certain Bandit toes the line," she said.

"Me? How can I stop Bandit from getting into trouble?" Iggy asked.

This was a mess. Even Iggy didn't trust Bandit. "Maybe Rihanna can leave her bedroom door open a bit, and you can tell her if Bandit escapes or something."

"I'm not going to escape, not when I have a warm place to sleep."

"I hope not."

Once we gathered our things, Jaxson and I left. As was our usual arrangement, he walked me home—two buildings away. For a change, I didn't have to kiss him goodnight in the hallway.

"Come on in."

"It's not too late," he said. "Care to watch a movie?"

I smiled. "I'd love to."

As was his habit, he made popcorn and grabbed us some beer while I picked the movie. It was a little strange not having Iggy making snide comments on the side. Just as Jaxson came out of the kitchen with the bowl of popcorn and our drinks, my cell rang.

I couldn't imagine who would be calling this late in the evening. When I checked the caller ID, I didn't recognize the number. "Hello?"

"Glinda, this is Shawn Shields."

My shoulders sagged. He was calling to tell all the cast members that the movie was over. "Yes, Mr. Shields?"

"Call me Shawn." His cheery tone surprised me. "I don't know if you heard, but Samuel confessed to killing Janet."

I had to pretend as if I didn't know. "Really? I never would have guessed." Yes, my comment sounded forced.

"I couldn't believe it either, but that is the reason for my call."

Here it comes. "Yes?"

"I've met your fiancé, and I was wondering if he might be willing to step in and take the role of Ivan Maynard."

I had no words. All I could do was hand Jaxson the phone. It certainly wasn't my call.

CHAPTER NINE

"Who's calling?" Jaxson mouthed.

"It's the director."

Jaxson's brows scrunched as he took the offered phone. "Hello?"

Shawn Shields must have talked for two minutes straight before Jaxson said anything. While he listened, I munched on the popcorn.

"I need to think about it.... Sure. I'll contact you tomorrow." Jaxson disconnected and looked at me. "Can you believe he wants me to act in a movie?"

Jaxson didn't sound as if he wanted to give it a go. "He does know you have no experience, right?"

"Yes, but he said they would cut down the role a bit to accommodate my inexperience."

I stilled. "What about the sexier scenes with Lynn Lurch? She was Alexa's understudy."

"I'd have to ask them to fade to black," he said. "I'm not making out with anyone but you."

I smiled. "You say the sweetest things. I wonder how Bethany will react to the news? Though if Gloria Vega kills Alexa in the movie, she should go to jail, and then poor Dr. Maynard won't have anyone. This isn't a love story, is it?"

"Maybe not."

"What are you going to do?" I asked.

"Now that I've had a moment, I don't think it's worth the hassle. Besides, I'm not an actor. What was the man thinking asking me to be in a movie?"

"No offense, but he's probably desperate," I said.

"Thanks." He winked to indicate he knew what I meant.

"Without Samuel Lipstein, will many people even pay to see the movie? Probably not, but if he posts your handsome face everywhere, every theater will be sold out."

"You are funny." Jaxson grabbed some popcorn and washed it down with beer.

Since I wasn't capable of forgetting about Shawn's offer, all the possibilities swam in my brain. "On second thought, I think you should consider taking the role."

"Why is that?"

"Think about it. If Samuel Lipstein isn't a

warlock, maybe he was hypnotized and told to confess. Someone like Hugo could probably make me confess to a murder."

Jaxson leaned back. "Are you saying I should go through with this so I can investigate Janet's murder?"

"Yes! And I'll be there, as will Penny. I bet between the three of us, and possibly our other more talented friends, we can figure out who killed Janet for real."

Jaxson said nothing for a minute. "If we agree to this, I'd like to tell Steve our plan."

"I have no problem with that, but he might say he already has the killer locked up."

Jaxson took another drink of his beer. "Do you really think he'll say for sure that Samuel is guilty if Steve doesn't have any evidence?"

"You have a point. He let Shawn Shields go even though Shawn had a motive to kill Janet. Steve just didn't have any physical evidence."

My cell rang. "Uh-oh. It's Gertrude. What is up with the late night calls this evening? I thought she went to bed early." Gertrude Poole was Levy's grandmother and possibly our most powerful witch in town.

"It must be important," Jaxson said. "Answer it."

"Gertrude, hello. Is everything all right?"

"I don't think so."

That didn't sound good. "Can I put you on speaker? Jaxson is here with me."

"Yes, please."

When she didn't say anything, I prodded her. "Can we help you?"

"I had a premonition tonight. You are in that movie they're shooting in town, right?"

"Yes." She probably learned about the Samuel's arrest, or else she just knew about it.

"I saw a large black cloud over the park."

I relaxed. "Yes, that would be because one of the leads was murdered a few days ago."

"No. This is about the future."

I looked over at Jaxson who leaned over my phone to make sure she could hear him. "Gertrude, this is Jaxson. Are you saying there is going to be another death?"

"It's possible. I have to interpret my premonitions, and I'm not always accurate, but I did see your face and Glinda's."

Chills raced down my arm. "Why would anyone want to harm us?" I asked.

"I wish I were a fortune teller, but I'm not. I just have premonitions that are subject to my interpretation. I'm sorry. I called to warn you to be careful. I want you to stay safe."

"Thank you. I appreciate the warning," I said.

"Goodnight, you two."

I wanted to ask her more about what she had seen, but I knew Gertrude well enough to know she told us all she intended to. I turned to Jaxson. "Okay, that was one of the stranger conversations I've had with her. And I've had some doozies. What do you think?"

"After that conversation, I will for sure say no to the director's offer. I can't risk you being harmed, because of something I did."

I figure he'd say that. "I get it, but her premonition might have nothing to do with the movie."

"I realize that, but what if it does?" he asked.

"I should tell Shawn what Gertrude told us, but he won't believe it unless he's into the occult."

"Probably true. I'm sure he can find someone else to take the role if he tries hard enough."

I munched on some more popcorn. "Suppose he does? I know Gertrude said she saw us in her mind's eye, but this new person could be in danger too—again, assuming the big cloud over the park means what she saw is connected to the movie." I leaned back, my mind spinning. "You know what? I will mention that to Shawn. If he doesn't believe me, at least I tried. I'd feel guilty if anyone else died because I kept my mouth shut."

Jaxson gathered me in his arms. "You are a good person, Glinda Goodall, but you can't save everyone."

"No, but I can try."

The call from Jaxson to Shawn turning down the offer to star in the movie had not been well received, which made me think the director wasn't going to give up so easily.

"I wouldn't take no for an answer either if I were Shawn. The movie needs a leading man." I leaned over and kissed Jaxson on the cheek. "Keep researching the cast members, but my diner scene is being reshot today. I have to go."

"With Lynn playing Nurse Alexa?"

"Yes."

"Who's playing Lynn's part?" he asked.

"I don't know. Actually, I'm not sure she will be replaced, but if she is, it's not like it's a big time commitment. I can think of a lot of people who could do a good job."

"Be careful out there."

"I will."

Iggy was somewhere with Bandit. If the movie had been canceled, it might be for the best. We'd drive Bandit across the state, and then Iggy could go back to obsessing about his seagull. Interesting that he hadn't had any Tippy sightings in the last few days. That led me to believe that Iggy might be the one who was taunting Tippy.

I entered the diner set where things appeared to be back to normal. I was dying to find out what everyone was thinking regarding Samuel Lipstein's confession. One of the cast members had to know something.

A woman I didn't recognize was wearing a similar waitress outfit to mine, and I couldn't help but wonder where the director found her. No time like the present to find out.

I walked up to her. "Hi, I'm Glinda, and I play Stella in the movie. You must be replacing Lynn Lurch."

"Yes, I'm Lisa Pena. Hi."

Pena? "Are you related to Chris, the screenwriter?"

Her face turned red. "Yes. Chris is my brother. I couldn't believe it when he called and said there was an opening. This is my dream come true."

Had he told her that she didn't have many more lines than I did? "That's great."

Shawn Shields clapped his hands. "Places, everyone. We're going to continue where we left off. Afterward, when we find a replacement for Samuel, we'll shoot all the scenes he has been in."

I wanted to ask what would happen if Steve thought that Samuel Lipstein might be covering for someone—like Bethany. Maybe the actor was in love with the actress for real and believed she'd killed Janet. To save her from a life in prison, he decided to confess.

I immediately stopped that train of thought. Other than in the movies, would anyone really do that, especially if they didn't know the other person very well?

Wait a minute. Being actors, they might have worked together before, so they might know each other well—very well. I hoped Jaxson had the chance to cross reference their parts.

On the other hand, maybe Chris Pena knew how much his sister wanted to be in a movie and decided to create an opening by killing Janet. Nah, that was a bit too farfetched. I was letting what Gertrude told us about the black cloud over the movie influence my thoughts.

The director was with Lynn, showing her where she needed to stand. At some point, I should tell him about the doom and gloom prediction that Gertrude prophesied. Even if he laughed at me, I'd feel better that I told him.

When it was my turn to take Nurse Alexa's order, it seemed a bit strange, but I pushed through it. The shot took less than a half an hour, for which I was grateful.

I never had the chance to speak with Shawn Shields about the prophesy since he rushed off to the other set, taking Lynn with him. There was always tomorrow.

As I stepped outside to return to the office, my body went left toward the sheriff's office instead of crossing the street to our office. I really wanted to know what evidence Steve had on Samuel Lipstein—not that he'd tell me.

The moment I entered his office, shouts were coming from Steve's office.

"Glinda, what an interesting outfit. Back to waitressing?" Pearl asked.

I hoped she hadn't forgotten that I was in the movie. "No, this is my movie costume." I nodded to the back. "What is all the shouting about?"

"It sounds like the hunky actor, Samuel, is not happy about something."

"You don't know what it's about?"

She lifted one shoulder. "Just stand here for a minute, and you'll figure it out."

I couldn't make out most of what they were saying, other than the actor was upset. Then he shouted something about him not killing anyone. I turned back to Pearl. "Were my sources wrong when I heard he'd confessed?"

I knew they weren't wrong, but I asked anyway.

"Oh, he confessed all right, but apparently he's changed his mind. That's all I know."

The image of a few people returning to town with little to no memory of what had happened to them shot into my head. Since a person of magic was involved in those cases, and a person of magic was involved now, I might be able to shed some light on things. I was about to insist that I speak with Steve when Samuel Lipstein charged into the main office area. Steve followed him, his hands on his hips. That was an interesting turn of events.

Samuel barely glanced my way as he shot passed me. He jerked open the front door and rushed out. I immediately spun around and faced Steve. "What was that about?"

"I'm not sure, but how about coming back to my office. I want to pass an idea by you."

This was a change. Usually, I had to beg him to let me help. I trotted after him, hoping that Iggy and Bandit hadn't cloaked themselves again and snuck into the sheriff's office. If I tripped over them, I'd be quite angry.

I pulled up a chair. "I take it that you couldn't find

any evidence against Samuel Lipstein that he killed Janet?"

"No. I knew it was too good to be true that he'd just come in here and confess."

Before I delved into my theory, I wanted to see where he was on the idea that magic was involved. "I take it Elissa explained the condition of Janet's body?"

"Yes, and I know she asked for your opinion—which she values."

A thrill raced up my spine. "That's nice to hear."

"She wasn't able to put magic as the cause of death, which is why I only have a preliminary report, but Elissa doesn't think she'll find an answer."

"That's too bad. She did say it was murder, right?"

He flashed me a smile. "Yes. We all agree that someone killed the actress. Who do you think murdered Janet? You must have an idea."

"I have too many suspects to pick just one. One thing I'm certain of is that whoever killed her was a very powerful witch or warlock."

"That's what Elissa said. Did you contact Levy?" Steve asked.

"I did, but he's never heard of anything quite like this before. That doesn't mean the brain drain can't be done. It's just that Levy can't explain how it was accomplished. What I do know is that we need to tread carefully."

"I couldn't agree more."

I filled him in on what Gertrude told us. "The director asked Jaxson to take Samuel's place as Dr. Maynard, but we decided it might be too dangerous. I'm just glad I only have to be in the diner scene where the front and side walls are glass. That way no one would dare harm me."

Steve nodded. "I'd like to know your take on Samuel's confession. Does it remind you of anything?"

"Funny you should ask that. When Andorra went missing for a while, she was hypnotized and did exactly what the person told her to do."

Steve pointed a finger at me. "That was my recollection, which is why I didn't find any physical evidence that ties Samuel Lipstein to Janet's death. While I have no idea if he is a warlock, his demeanor changed completely from one day to the next."

"Like the spell that made him confess must have worn off."

"Precisely."

"Give me some time to do some research on this. While I have a feeling that Hugo has the ability to pull off something like this, he wouldn't do that. He seems quite honorable."

"I agree. He might not even know there is a movie going on," Steve said.

I chuckled. "You might be right."

"Can Levy help with this false confession?"

"You better watch out. I think you are developing psychic skills. I was just thinking about contacting him."

His eyebrows rose. "At times, I wish I had mad magical skills. It might make my job easier."

"Totally," I said.

"Let me know what he says."

"Will do."

CHAPTER TEN

ONE PLUS to Steve releasing Samuel Lipstein was that the director wouldn't have to find a replacement for the actor. The only scenes that would need to be reshot were ones that involved the new Alexa.

Shawn was probably worried that the cast might not believe that Lipstein was innocent. His confession would make it hard for most people to be certain it was all a mistake, especially since they hadn't been told about the supposed hypnosis.

Personally, I was confident someone else had killed Janet mostly because no one claimed that Samuel Lipstein was a warlock, though the possibility we were all wrong existed. I'd heard that with practice, a person could hide his abilities.

On my way back to the office I rang up Levy again.

"This is a surprise. Do you have another crime that needs to be solved?"

I always enjoyed hearing the cheer in his voice. "As a matter of fact I do."

"Perhaps I should move to Witch's Cove. Your town seems to be the hotbed of intrigue."

I chuckled. "It does, doesn't it?"

"What do you need?"

I crossed the street and walked toward our office. "Something happened that is similar to what I've seen before." I explained how Samuel Lipstein confessed to murdering Janet yesterday, and then today, he claimed he didn't know anything about the murder."

"He has no idea what happened?" Levy asked.

"No, but apparently, he sounded rather robotic when he confessed and was then very animated when he woke up the next morning. I'm thinking someone put a spell on him."

"That sure sounds like it. You've been involved in a few incidences like this before, though."

"I know, but I don't think we ever learned exactly how reprogramming or brainwashing a person worked. I know that Hugo can get people to tell the truth, but this is different."

"It does sound as if this Samuel was under hypnosis."

I reached the office and climbed the steps. "Does hypnosis require a spell? Or should I ask if the person doing the hypnosis needs to relax the affected person first, like when a psychologist performs it?"

"Sometimes yes, sometimes no. I've seen it done both ways. In this case, if the man doesn't remember anything, I would assume it was a spell in which this actor was completely unaware of what was occurring."

I was worried that might be the case. "That will make it harder to learn who this witch or warlock is."

"True. I'd say keep watching the interaction of the people in the movie. Something will pop up that gives you a clue."

"I hope so." After I thanked him for his time—again—I entered the office to find Jaxson and Rihanna doing their thing.

"Hey," he said. "How did the shoot go?"

"The shoot went well, but it was my interaction with Steve that was more interesting. Let me grab a drink, and I will regale you two with what I know."

After I finished pouring a glass of tea, I returned to the living room. I spotted Iggy but not Bandit. "Where is your friend?"

"He wanted to go back to the scene of the crime and see what he could learn."

Steve had already processed the trailer, so I doubt

he could ruin anything. I was pretty sure Bandit didn't have a key, so how would he be able to enter the place? Hmm. Then again, raccoons seemed to find their way into impossible places. "Bandit didn't ask you to join him in his search?"

"No."

I found that interesting. "I'm glad, because I could use your help here."

Iggy crawled onto the coffee table. "What do you need to know?"

Jaxson wheeled his office chair over to the sofa area. "We're all ears."

I explained that Steve let Samuel Lipstein go because the confessor claimed he never admitted to killing anyone—and because Steve had no evidence that tied Samuel to the crime.

"I thought he signed a confession," Jaxson said.

"He did, but Steve understands that this is Witch's Cove. Apparently, Samuel was robotic acting when he first came in, and trust me, he was quite animated when he left."

"Are you thinking someone put a spell on him?" Rihanna asked.

"That's my guess. I conferred with Levy, and he thought the same thing."

"How does that help us find the killer?" Jaxson asked.

"It doesn't, which makes me think we need to enlist the aid of the director."

Jaxson's eyes widened. "You think he'd help?"

"I would think he'd want to do something if there is a killer still on the loose."

"What did Shawn say when you mentioned Gertrude's theory?" Jaxson asked.

"I didn't tell him yet. He rushed off to the other set before I had the chance."

Jaxson glanced at the clock. "What time do they wrap for the day?"

I was usually only needed to work in the morning. "I don't know, but if we look out the window, I can tell if there is any activity inside the fake diner. They are shooting at the other location outside of town at the moment, but they might return to this side of town."

"Do you want me to keep watch on the fake diner and tell you if the crew returns?" Iggy asked.

"I appreciate the offer, but you can't stay cloaked for hours. Besides, people will be rushing all over the place. Someone might step on you."

"Okay." I hated how dejected he sounded.

"How about if I ask Genevieve and Hugo to tele-port in and out of both locations to see when the director is free to chat?" I suggested.

"What if someone runs into an invisible Hugo?" Iggy asked.

"I think he can move out of the way before that happens."

"Okay. I'll go ask him." Before I could agree or disagree, Iggy sped out the cat door. Two weeks ago, Jaxson had installed a small lizard door in the Hex and Bones entrance that allowed Iggy to come and go. At the time, he had been so excited to be able to visit Hugo and possibly Ruby on his own. Then Bandit arrived, and I don't think Iggy had used his special entrance since.

"Do you really think the director can help?" Rihanna asked. "It's not like he'll know who has magic and who doesn't."

"No, he won't know that, but I'm hoping he has an idea who might have wanted Janet dead." Besides maybe himself. And no, I don't think he could have killed her.

"Fingers crossed," she said.

"Since it's going to take Iggy a bit to chat with Hugo, how about we take another look at the list of possible suspects?" I asked.

"Sure, but we still need to figure out a way to discover who has powers and who doesn't?" Rihanna asked.

"I know, but since we are in the dark about that at

the moment, we should list everyone and their motive for wanting Janet dead, and then we can eliminate those who have no powers at a later date."

"I say, go for it," Jaxson said. "We know Bethany is a witch. She might know who else is."

There was a flaw in his thinking. "I'm a witch, and yet I don't know who is *special* and who isn't—as Iggy would say."

"True," he replied.

I went up to the white board. "Even though the director had motive, he doesn't have any magic—or so we believe. I'm guessing the same goes for Samuel Lipstein."

"We should focus on whether the screenwriter, Janet's replacement, or the fake diner owner have any abilities," Rihanna said.

"I totally agree. The diner owner, Leah Samson, who is played by Kristen Revere, only has had a few lines so far. Her big scenes come in the second half of the movie. Let's suppose Kristen is a witch. What would be her motive for killing Janet?"

Jaxson looked at me. "I can't say." He pulled out a piece of paper. "I have the list of the actors I found on the Internet, but it might not be up-to-date."

"Yeah, sorry. I keep forgetting to ask Shawn for it."

"You have a lot on your mind."

As did Shawn. I listed a few of the other people in the movie, including Lynn's replacement, but they mostly had minor roles. It was possible there had been bad blood between Janet and someone else on another movie, but we'd have to wait until we had the final list.

We spent another hour hashing out possible suspects and motives. Out of the corner of my eye, I spotted Hugo holding Iggy. They'd just appeared in our office. Even after the numerous times Hugo had teleported, his sudden appearance startled me.

"Hugo said they just finished one scene and are getting ready to do another," Iggy said. "They aren't at the diner but at the other set."

"Thank you, Hugo. I appreciate your help." I turned to Jaxson. "Do you want to come with me to the set?"

"Sure. You're not afraid, are you?"

"No, or I wasn't until you asked."

Hugo placed Iggy on the coffee table and then disappeared. I assumed he'd teleported back to the Hex and Bones.

"Iggy, come over here and tell me what else Hugo said." Rihanna could sense when Iggy felt left out.

While she kept him busy, we slipped out. We took Jaxson's truck and drove to the main set. Thankfully,

Shawn Shields was still inside with a handful of his crew. Either they were finished, or they were transitioning to another scene.

He spun around. "Glinda, Jaxson. What are you doing here?"

It was time to explain who we really were. "I didn't see the need to mention it before, but now that Janet is dead, I'd like to offer you our help. Jaxson and I are amateur sleuths." I held up a hand. Because we weren't licensed, people often thought we were hacks. "Before you say anything, we've helped the sheriff solve many murders. Why? Because I'm a witch."

"Just because Bethany and Janet portray witches, it doesn't mean witchcraft exists."

I wasn't surprised at his response. "Whether you believe me or not, I am a witch. Bottom line is that someone killed Janet Wood. My fiancé is a whiz at computers, and he'd like to see who might have interacted with her in the past. That could help us figure out who had a motive to kill her."

"Interesting. What do you think I can do?"

"We'd like the names of the current cast members. A few are different from when the list was first published. And no, we don't charge a fee for our work." The potential client usually asked.

Shawn pressed his lips together as his gaze ran up and down our bodies, though I wasn't sure what he hoped to learn. "I'll ask Chuck to get you the list by tomorrow at the latest. Just so you know, many of the actors have worked together in the past as have the staff. I'm not sure you'll find much motive for murder there, though."

"We still want to try." I knew Shawn's assistant, Chuck, and the makeup artist, Olivia Richards, but I didn't know any of the cameramen. Tomorrow, I might have to rectify that.

The director stood. "Now, if you'll excuse me, I have a lot of work to do. We have to redo many of the scenes."

"Of course." Since I didn't want him to think I was a total kook, I didn't tell him about Gertrude's psychic moment. Maybe I'd bring it up later.

After we left, I waited until we were in Jaxson's truck before I brought up my idea. "Do you think Steve asked Hugo and Genevieve to snoop again?"

"Anything's possible, but what could he hope to find? The killer has completed his job, or are you thinking someone plans to pick off the cast one at a time?"

I shivered at that thought. "No, or at least I hope not."

A few minutes later, we arrived at the office where I found Rihanna reading a book.

She looked up. "How did it go?"

"The director will send us the updated list of cast members by tomorrow."

"Great, now all you need is an insider to ask questions," Rihanna said.

I hadn't thought of that. "Do you mean like Samuel Lipstein?"

She smiled. "Not exactly. I was thinking more on the lines of the make-up girl. You know people tell their hair dressers everything!"

"Oh, that is a great idea. How about tomorrow, I invite Olivia out to lunch and you join us?"

"I only have one photo class in the morning and then I'm free, but why ask me? Olivia might think it's strange to have someone not associated with the film be there."

"You're my cousin. We'll eat at the Tiki Hut Grill. Trust me, it will seem natural."

"I'm happy to join you, but what about Penny?" Rihanna asked. "Since she is a cast member, your makeup girl will think that is more natural."

She had a point, but Rihanna was better at reading minds. Penny's forte was knowing if a person lied. "I'll see what Penny's schedule is, but if she can't make it, can I count on you? Not that I don't thoroughly enjoy your company, but I can always use a mind reader."

My cousin laughed. "I'm being used. I get it."

"I'll text you tomorrow if I need back up, okay?"

"You got it."

CHAPTER ELEVEN

"Olivia, aren't you even a little scared to be alone with the actors?" I asked the makeup artist.

"Why should I be scared?"

I might be overreacting, but no one could be sure of the motive behind Janet's death. "I don't know. Maybe because there might be a killer on the loose?" That came out too snarky. "Look, I doubt he'll strike again, but he could."

Olivia lowered her gaze. "I'm a nobody. There is no reason to harm me."

"I know. Me, too, but it doesn't hurt to be careful," I said.

She bit her bottom lip. "Maybe I'll buy a can of mace."

I doubt that would stop a warlock from either hypnotizing her or killing her, but I wasn't going to

voice that opinion. That would require a long explanation of the previous events, and I'm not sure she'd
believe me anyway.

"Good idea."

"Say, Olivia, when you do the actor's makeup, I
bet some are pretty chatty, right?" Penny asked.

While Rihanna was more reliable at knowing
what a person was thinking, my cousin was right. It
made more sense for Penny to be there since she was
a member of the cast. Besides, when I mentioned
having lunch with Olivia in order to get the down low
on the actors, Penny was really excited to join us. If
I'd been thinking straight, I would have had both of
them there.

"You have no idea," Olivia said.

I grinned. "Did anyone chat about Janet?"

"Not a lot. All the women wanted to talk about
how hot Samuel Lipstein was. I don't think many
people liked Janet. I take that back. Samuel liked her
for a while, but then he didn't."

That had potential. "Did he say what happened to
make him change his mind?"

"Sort of. Did you know that he and the woman
who plays Gloria were kind of a thing in another
movie that Shawn directed?"

"I didn't know. So they were an item?" Jaxson had
unearthed some information to indicate they might

have been, but it wouldn't serve any purpose to tell her that.

"Absolutely. To be fair, a lot of leading ladies and leading men get carried away with their roles and think they are in love. When the movie wraps, they go their separate ways. Some are upset, others are not —or so the actors say."

"Is that what happened to Samuel and..."

"Bethany Aldrich who plays Gloria Vega? Yes."

"When were they in this other movie together?"

Olivia blew out a breath. "That's hard to say. Maybe two movies ago? I've done about six movies with Shawn, and time flies."

"I can relate. Did you think their relationship was for real?" Olivia was about my age, so her opinion might be a little biased. Young people saw love everywhere.

"I thought so."

Penny sipped her soda. "When Bethany and Samuel signed up to be in this movie, did they both know that Janet would try to steal Samuel away from Bethany in the movie?"

"They must have. Samuel told me that everyone receives the script beforehand."

"Did you read the script?"

She chuckled. "No. I'm just the makeup lady. Shawn tells me what to do, and I do it. This isn't some sci-fi movie where I have to create monsters. Someday, maybe."

She was a dreamer. Good to know. "I heard that Janet put an actual love spell on Samuel, and that when he found out, he wasn't happy."

"He might have been upset, but it was Bethany who was livid," Olivia said.

Interesting. From Olivia's response, she seemed to believe that magic existed. "Did Bethany tell you she was angry at Janet for doing the spell, or did she just appear agitated, and you assumed it was because Janet was trying to steal Samuel away?"

"No, she told me."

I leaned closer. "So you do believe in witchcraft and spells and such?"

She dipped her chin. "No. That is poppycock."

That wasn't what she implied a moment ago. Was that because she had done something to Janet and feared we might realize she was a killer?

"Both Penny and I are witches, and I can assure you that spells can hypnotize people and even kill people."

"Shut the door," the young girl said.

I hope that Penny was sensing whether Olivia was telling the truth or not. "I'm being serious. You said that Samuel didn't seem to like Janet when the movie started, right?"

"Yes, but he was too much of a gentleman to complain. Some actors are nice like that. Others, not so much."

Perhaps our makeup artist wanted to believe he was a free agent and was hoping to snag his attention. Samuel was older than her by a few years, but that might not have bothered her, especially if she'd worked with him in previous films. While it seemed as if Olivia was this innocent woman, could she really be a witch with a murderous streak in disguise? I noticed that whenever she said Samuel's name, she'd swoon. That alone, however, proved nothing.

From my perspective, Samuel seemed attracted to Bethany, but they were good actors, so it was hard to know for sure. If I had wanted Samuel for myself, I might have considered killing Bethany, not Janet.

Penny placed a hand on my arm. "Are you okay?"

I drew my attention back to the task at hand. "Yeah, sure." I smiled. Daydreaming in the middle of an investigation was a dangerous trait.

Olivia pushed back her chair. "I need to go. Shawn will be upset if I'm late. If I don't do the makeup, there will be no filming."

"Of course. Thanks for joining us. We'll have to do this another time."

"For sure."

I'd already told her that I'd treat her to lunch.

Olivia grabbed her purse and sweater and took off. As soon as she was out the door, I turned to Penny. "What did you think?"

"She seems sweet."

"Right. Too sweet. Was she telling the truth about everything?"

Penny chuckled. "No one tells the truth about everything."

"You know what I mean."

Penny nodded. "She believes in witches, but before you say, *aha*, many people don't want to admit they have magic or believe in magic."

"I figured that was the case, but once I said we were witches, I'd hoped she would have admitted something." I polished off the rest of my tea. "Does she seem like the type who could kill someone, though?" I asked.

"Really? We spent about thirty minutes with her. Off the cuff, I'd say no, but she did have a fascination with Samuel."

"That's what I thought. I'd like to know if it was more of an obsession or a mere infatuation." Before Penny could give me her thoughts, my cell dinged. "I hope this is what I asked for." I checked the screen. "Good. It's from Shawn's assistant. He sent the list of all of the actors' and stage hands' real names."

"Great. Now Jaxson can finish connecting the dots."

"Totally." I immediately forwarded the email to him.

Penny pulled out money for her meal. "Off to the set. I have to sit in the doctor's waiting room, but in this scene, I don't interact with Samuel. Such excitement." She flipped back her hair.

I laughed at her antics. I stood and then hugged her goodbye. "Don't flirt with him."

"Me? Never." She stilled. "Are you thinking the killer plans to take down all women who look twice at the man?"

"Maybe, but Janet's murder might have had nothing to do with Samuel and everything to do with Shawn's illegal theft of that movie short."

"It's possible."

"I'm not sure I believe Shawn's whole story about the theft. I think more might be involved here," I said.

Penny sucked in a breath. "Does that mean we're overlooking an important person?"

"Maybe, but who?"

"This wronged movie guy—the one who Shawn stole from? Do you know if Shawn has ever met the man? And I mean face-to-face, not just via email."

"I have no idea. Why?"

"If someone had taken my one big idea and won an award and a movie contract because of it, I'd want revenge," she said.

Oh, my. "Do you think it's possible that this Benson McDaniels might have harmed Janet to get back at Shawn?"

"Maybe."

I scrunched up my nose. "That throws a wrench into the whole case. Personally, I would have killed Shawn, though that might have been too obvious. Instead of Janet, I would have gone after Samuel. He would be harder to replace—assuming I wanted to bring as much pain to the thieving director as I could."

"Maybe it was a matter of opportunity. Benson McDaniels' plan might have been to kill the leading man—assuming his goal was to exact the most emotional pain as possible on Shawn—but Samuel could have been busy with Bethany at the time, so he targeted Janet." Penny smiled, obviously pleased with her analysis. "But that's just a guess."

"One that has a lot of potential, I might add. I wonder if Jaxson can find a picture of this Benson person. He could be a cameraman or an extra on the set for all we know."

She smiled. "I do love your imagination. It's no

wonder you don't always sleep well at night. I gotta go."

"Have fun office sitting."

She stuck her tongue out at me and then left. After I paid the bill, I went back to the office.

When I entered, not only was Jaxson there, but so was Bandit and Iggy. I didn't know where Rihanna was. "Hi, guys."

"How was lunch?" Jaxson asked.

"Good." I tossed my bag and then my sweater on the sofa and sat down.

I told all three of them what Olivia said. "Penny didn't think she was telling the truth about everything."

"What did she lie about?" Jaxson asked.

"Not a lie per se, but Olivia contradicted herself about witchcraft. She implied she believed in it, but when questioned, Olivia denied it."

"That doesn't make her a killer."

Bandit moved closer to the sofa. "Do you want me to keep an eye on her?"

I blew out a breath. Did I? He could remain cloaked, but for how long? "I like the idea of you snooping around, but let's see who might need watching the most."

"Okay, but Bethany seems really happy of late."

"Why is that do you suppose? Because her

nemesis was dead?" I doubted a raccoon would possess a lot of insight into a person's motivation, but Bandit was magical. He might have more human qualities than I'd given him credit.

"I heard her tell Samuel that she was happy they had a new Alexa."

Aha! That might mean something. "Did she say why?"

"Just that she thinks Lynn is a better actress than Janet," Bandit said.

Was that all? "I didn't know that Lynn had a lot of experience." I turned back to Jaxson. "Can you look into Lynn's acting history too? I'd be interested to see if maybe she has more movies under her belt than Janet. That might give Lynn a reason to kill Janet Wood—professional jealousy. Her death might not be related to Samuel Lipstein in any way."

"Got it."

"Before I forget, do you think you can find an image of Benson McDaniels—the guy who wrote the movie that Shawn stole?"

"A lot of people are in Google images, and that's the problem. There could be ten Benson McDaniels, and it might be hard to know which is the one you are looking for, but give me a second to check." Jaxson did a search and was done in about a minute.

"As I suspected, there are quite a few people with his same name."

"Do any of them indicate they are screenwriters?"

"No, but I'll cross reference all of the movies with the actors. Something might come up, but that will take a lot of time. These actors work hard."

"Do what you can. Thanks." I returned my focus to the two familiars staring up at me. "Bandit, I heard you trashed Samuel's trailer at one time. Why was that?"

"I didn't want to do it."

I huffed out a laugh. "Then why did you?"

"Janet made me."

My eyes widened. I hope he wasn't about to say he was hypnotized. "Did she say why?"

"Yes. It was because she was jealous of Bethany."

That was interesting. "I think Bethany and I might have to have a chat."

"No!" Jaxson said. "We don't know that she didn't kill Janet."

"He's right," Bandit said. "I need to spy some more before you approach her."

The raccoon did seem rather determined, and who was I to stop him? "Okay, but you should wait until after they've finished shooting for the day. And speaking of chatting with cast members, I think I'll approach Samuel first. While he did confess to murder, from his confused response the next day, I'm pretty sure that he is innocent."

"That sounds good," Bandit said. "You keep him busy while I listen to what Bethany has to say."

"Bandit, unless Bethany is with someone, she won't be talking. I bet that as soon as I finish chatting with Samuel, he'll rush over to her trailer and tell her what we discussed. That's when you'll need to listen."

Bandit lowered his head. "I bet he doesn't know who killed Janet, which means he might be afraid to confide in Bethany."

"That would mean he suspects her." I had to give the raccoon credit. He wasn't as simple minded as I first thought. "Let's see what happens. If Samuel seeks out Bethany's counsel, I'd like you to be there."

"You got it."

Iggy spun around. "I'll tell Hugo to be the park bodyguard. Just give a yell if you have any problems, and he'll help," he told me.

I smiled. "What a wonderful idea."

Hopefully, it wouldn't be necessary.

CHAPTER TWELVE

"I APPRECIATE you taking the time to chat with me," I told Samuel Lipstein.

"Sure." He unlocked his trailer door and motioned me inside. Now I was glad that Iggy had asked Hugo to stand watch—assuming he'd shown up. I swallowed my anxiety. I trusted Iggy, or rather Hugo to be there—albeit in his invisible form.

Samuel motioned that I take a seat on the sofa. Since the trailer wasn't exactly spacious, being in there with him was a little uncomfortable, but I had to remind myself that he wasn't a warlock—or so I believed.

Oh, how I wish there was some test I could perform to tell if a person had magic or not, other than asking Iggy to shout at the person to see if he responded. That method wasn't always foolproof, however.

"I imagine you've heard that my fiancé and I run a kind of detective agency."

"Shawn mentioned it."

I waited for him to ask me about Janet and whether I had any clues to the killer's identity, but he didn't say anything.

"Despite your confession to the sheriff, I believe that you didn't kill her."

To my surprise, the man didn't react to my statement. Or was he being the consummate actor? On the other hand, he might assume everyone believed his arrest was ridiculous, so of course, I'd believe him.

"How can you be so sure?" His even, low tone almost sounded threatening. Whoops. My assumption might have been wrong. What I wouldn't give to be a human lie detector like Penny right now—or read thoughts like Rihanna.

My pulse shot up. "A warlock or witch killed her. We believe from the way you reacted to finding out that you'd signed a confession that you had been hypnotized and told to sign the paper. I assume you aren't a warlock, right? Or did I read the signs wrong?" I put as much confidence into my words as possible and hoped I'd read him correctly.

His head shake appeared to be one of denial. No

one likes to think they'd been fooled. "Seriously? A warlock? I can guarantee you that I have no magical powers, though they would come in handy when I need to learn my lines better." He paused. "Do you really think I was hypnotized?"

Did this mean he believed in witchcraft? Perhaps Bethany had convinced him witches were real. "Yes, which is partially why I'm here."

The tight control he'd been exhibiting a moment ago seemed to disappear. "Look, if you are here to find out who hypnotized me, I have no idea. And that's the truth."

That wasn't what I wanted to hear, but I believed him. "Who were you with right before you went to the sheriff's office?"

"No one." He stilled and then looked off to the side. "No wait, I'd finished filming for the day. Maybe you can ask to see the video in case there was some evil-looking person in the background."

It wasn't as if warlocks and witches wore tall pointy black hats, had long noses, and beady eyes. If I had to point a finger at someone, it would be one of the actors, cameramen, or extras who performed the spell. Shoot. That didn't narrow it down very much, did it? "I might do that."

He leaned forward. Samuel's demeanor seemed to change, maybe because for the first time in hours, he believed he'd found an ally. "Could someone hypnotize me without my knowledge, though?" he asked.

"Sadly, yes, but I can't say how exactly. Let me ask you, do you recall walking down the sidewalk before turning yourself in?"

"No. That's the crazy part. I remember Shawn calling it a wrap and then I walked back to my trailer."

"Alone?"

"No. Bethany and I walked back together, but she went her way, and I went mine. I wanted to grab my script to study. We had a lot of work to do what with Janet gone."

That made sense. "Then what?"

He shrugged. "Then nothing. I woke up in a jail cell. I was confused and then angry. I knew there had to have been a mistake."

And he made his dissatisfaction known to Steve. I heard that discussion. "That would be scary."

"You have no idea. I'd never been in a police station before, let alone locked in a jail cell. Trust me, that place stank."

Steve claimed he didn't want to make it too cushy. "Cells are supposed to be a deterrent. Hence the lumpy mattress and nasty conditions."

"You got that right."

"Do you have any theories about what happened to Janet Wood?"

"No. I mean, there were people who didn't like her or that raccoon of hers, but enough to kill? I wouldn't even want to guess who it could be."

"Have you worked with her before?"

"Sure, but since she didn't have a leading role when I did, we weren't in many or any big scenes together."

"So, you didn't know her very well?" I asked.

"Not until this film."

If I could read between the lines on what Bandit said, they had been intimate. "Can I ask how you knew where to look for the dirt on Shawn Shields?" He'd located the information about the stolen manuscript in Janet's trailer after she died.

"You won't believe me."

Uh-oh. Was he hypnotized again? "Try me."

"It was as if I had a person in my head telling me where to search. I know that sounds crazy. Heck, it is crazy, but within a matter of minutes I had found the documents that proved our director wasn't totally above-board with the studio. If the information had been that easy to locate, why didn't the sheriff find it when he processed her trailer?"

"He might not have realized what the documents were." Wait a minute. Were we talking about Janet's ghost here? I'd never heard of one sending messages to a non-magical person before, but I was no expert. "Where did you find the documents?"

"Inside her day planner. I went straight to the date this person in my head told me to go to, and I found it."

"I see. Since you two were working together on the film, could Janet have mentioned it to you at one point? Maybe when you were rehearsing a scene in her trailer?"

He seemed to think about it for a moment. "Not that I remember, but right now, anything is possible."

Since there probably wasn't much more he could tell me, I picked up my purse. "I'm sorry this happened to you, but if you see someone lurking in the background, let our sheriff know. He doesn't mind tracking down leads."

Steve wouldn't be happy with me if he knew I'd said that. Genevieve, however, would be thrilled to run down a lead.

"I will and thanks for believing me. This whole Janet thing has thrown me for a loop."

"I totally understand. Oh, there's one more thing I've been meaning to ask you." He nodded. "In the movie, Nurse Alexa wanted to have you fall in love with her instead of Gloria. For that to happen, she had to prepare a love potion. I'm sure the writer, the director, and everyone—including yourself—assumed the spell was just a movie device."

"That's true. And before you ask, when she said the words over her herb and spice mixture, I felt this overwhelming sense of warmth and calm overtake me. I'm more certain than ever that Janet put a real spell on me. And trust me, I never believed in that witch stuff before."

"Considering Janet was a witch, it makes sense."

"She said she was one, but I figured she was playing the role to the max. After the spell, I believed her."

"You should. Janet Wood was the real deal."

"I don't know if this is important, but I didn't like her all that much before the scene with the spell, but afterward, I felt a deep connection to her."

A connection, and falling in love, were two different things. But hey, potatoes, pot*a*toes. "I've heard that you and Bethany were dating. Did the spell affect your feelings for her?"

He half chuckled and broke eye contact. "I thought it wouldn't, but it did at first."

I didn't want to ask, but I had to. "Did Bethany suspect something had happened between you and Janet?"

"Very much so. I explained about the effect of the spell, but she said that love spells didn't exist."

I was a witch and didn't think love spells existed either. "You weren't able to convince her?"

"Not at first. I swore to her that there was nothing between me and Janet, but Bethany wasn't totally convinced." He threaded his fingers together, almost as if he was afraid of something. The white knuckles said a lot.

"Do you think Bethany had anything to do with Janet's death?"

"What? No. Never. Bethany is the sweetest woman alive."

From his near shout, he believed it. "Great. I just had to ask. Please tell Steve if you feel threatened or see anyone unusual hanging around."

"You think this person will kill again?"

"I don't know, but I'm staying alert." Before he questioned me further, I left.

Once outside, I waved to Hugo—wherever he was —to show him that I was okay. Now came the more interesting part. What would Samuel do next? If he and Bethany Aldrich were a couple, and if they had kissed and made up, I suspect he'd visit her. That was where Hugo and Bandit would play their part.

I walked back toward the office, content that my job was done for the day. Even though it was a little early for dinner, I was really hungry. I'd already called Aunt Fern and asked her what she knew about Janet's murder, but she said things had been quiet on the gossip front.

Inside the office, I found Iggy, Rihanna, and Jaxson. All three turned toward me.

"What did Samuel have to say?" Jaxson asked.

I told them everything and then looked at Iggy. "Bandit is sleuthing for us, isn't he?"

"Yes, but I told Hugo that he might have to teleport him inside Bethany's trailer."

"It's so nice to have a friend who has that talent. Did you ask Hugo to come over here afterward if the actors get together—assuming they do?"

He tilted his head. "What do you take me for?"

Ouch. I hadn't meant to offend him. "Of course, you did. Thank you." I turned to the others. "I'm starving, and Aunt Fern knows nothing."

Jaxson chuckled. "I think you know more than Dolly, so how about the Magic Wand Hotel?"

It was expensive, but I sensed Jaxson had an ulterior motive for wanting to eat there. "Since many of the actors are staying there, it might be interesting to see if any of them will share some gossip." I turned to Rihanna. "Do you want to join us?"

"Sure."

"What about me and Bandit?" Iggy asked rather indignantly.

"I would like to hear what he has to say, but I

don't know how long he's going to be gone. How about you wait for him here? I bet we're back before he returns."

Iggy cocked his head. "You're just saying that because you want to be by yourself."

Was he right? "You know that the fancy hotel frowns on pets in the dining room."

Iggy didn't answer. Instead he crawled underneath the sofa. I hoped that Iggy didn't tell Bandit to keep what he learned to himself just to spite me. Whatever. Sometimes there was no pleasing my familiar.

Jaxson, Rihanna, and I left. As we crossed the street, I glanced toward the park, wondering how Bandit was fairing.

"Do you think Samuel Lipstein is going to say something earth-shattering to Bethany?" Rihanna asked.

"I hope not. I believe he is innocent. It's Bethany that I am still questioning. I figure if he doesn't tell her much, then maybe he doesn't trust her. Samuel told me that she didn't forgive him quickly after Janet did the love spell," I said.

"Can you blame her? What would you do if Jaxson came in one day and said he'd fallen in love with another woman, but that it wasn't his fault, because some witchy siren put a love spell on him?"

That was a good question. "I'd find out who she was and talk with her."

"Talk?" Rihanna asked. "I know you trust Jaxson, but if that happened, we could ask Hugo to reprogram this woman. And by reprogram, I mean have him take away her power to ever do a spell again."

I chuckled. "I doubt he has that ability. If he did, he could take away the power of all magical beings who'd used their talents for evil."

"You might be right."

"Before we consider taking away someone's power forever, we need to be certain who hypnotized Samuel."

"Are you sure the same person who hypnotized him also killed Janet?" Jaxson asked.

"It makes sense they'd be the same person, but I have no proof."

"Good to know." Jaxson held open the Magic Wand Hotel door. "After you, ladies. By the way, no spell will make me fall out of love with you, Glinda."

"Aw. If we weren't in the lobby of a busy hotel, I'd kiss you."

He grinned. "I don't think anyone would mind."

CHAPTER THIRTEEN

UNFORTUNATELY, no one of interest had been at the hotel restaurant while the three of us were there. I suspected it was too early for many of the cast since most would still be filming. I hoped Bethany hadn't been needed on the set. Then Samuel couldn't have spoken with her.

When we returned to the office, Hugo, Bandit, and Iggy were all chatting—or rather Iggy was chatting and translating what Hugo said to Bandit.

"Hey, guys. Bandit, did you learn anything, or wasn't Bethany in her trailer?"

"She was there." Bandit pranced over to our seating area. Clearly, he'd figured out this was where all the action occurred. "The actor guy did as you thought he would. He visited his girlfriend and told her what you discussed. He seemed really happy that someone believed him about his confession being coerced—if that's the right word."

"It's good enough. Did they talk about who might have killed your host or anything about his hypnosis?"

Bandit looked over at Hugo. That kind of implied Hugo was with Bandit. "A little. Nothing new, though. Got any food? All that staying in one place makes me hungry."

I didn't have much since I fed Ruby before. "I'll see what I do have. I can pick up more food tomorrow."

"Great, thank you."

I didn't expect his polite response. Sadly, all I was able to scrounge up was some lettuce that had been earmarked for Iggy and my last can of tuna. Feeding all of these familiars was becoming rather expensive, but that was the price of paying for information, I guess.

I put what I had on a plate and carried it out. "Sorry for the slim pickings."

"This is good," Bandit said.

Iggy waddled over to me. "Is that my lettuce?"

"I'll buy you more tomorrow."

"Fine." Iggy looked over at Hugo who stood as still as a statue this whole time. "Hugo wants to know if you need him to help in any other way?"

"Thank you, Hugo. That's nice of you to ask. I wish I knew where we should go from here, but I don't. Not yet at least." I motioned for Jaxson and Rihanna to sit in our living room seating area. "Either of you have any suggestions what our next move should be?"

"I need another day to finish creating the chart that shows who worked with whom in the past. The problem as I see it is that just because two people acted in the same movie together doesn't mean they didn't like each other," Jaxson said. "On the contrary. They might have formed a bond."

"True. Even if Shawn wanted to cooperate, I doubt he's aware of the actors' interactions with each other, especially if it took place in the hotel or some-place else."

"Okay, Hugo. I'll tell her." Iggy came over to the coffee table and climbed up. "Hugo said he is going to keep an eye on the people in the park. He will ask Genevieve to stand watch over the hotel folks. If anyone leaves in the middle of the night, they will let you know."

I faced Hugo. "That is a great idea. Thank you."

"What can I do?" Bandit asked.

I couldn't help but wonder why he was being so helpful all of a sudden? I had to assume he liked being useful, or rather needed, for a change. It was possible

Bandit didn't want to move across the state and live with someone who might not really care for him. Right now, I couldn't dwell on that.

"As soon as I figure out what we need to do next, I'll see if you and Iggy can help."

"Okay." With that, Bandit slipped out the cat door.

"Why did he leave?" I asked Iggy.

"How would I know?"

As if Hugo needed to make sure Bandit didn't cause any trouble, he left too—only this time he actually used the door. Something strange was going on in the universe. I wonder if it had anything to do with the black cloud that Gertrude spoke about?

"I think we all need to sleep on this. Tomorrow might bring some clarity," I said. "I'm going to head out. Walk me home?" I asked Jaxson.

"Of course."

"Goodnight, Rihanna."

"Goodnight. Oh, Glinda, before you go, I want to ask you something."

"Sure?"

"Do you think your director would mind if I take some stills of him and the others during the filming?" Rihanna asked. "I don't have any classes tomorrow."

I didn't see where she was going with this. "We

can ask, but why would you want to, other than for the experience?"

She smiled. "I was thinking that I might catch someone in the background doing something they shouldn't. I figure it can't hurt."

I smiled. "All he can say is no. We'll tell him that you are a photography major and that if he wishes, you can post the photos on line for the cast to use if they want."

"Sounds like a plan."

"Great. How about we go together tomorrow morning? I'll introduce you. If he balks, I might tell him the truth."

"And say what? That I'm spying?" I nodded. "I like it."

"You're sure the director is innocent?" Jaxson asked.

"Of killing someone? Yes. I think the man is rather immoral if he stole someone's movie and claimed it for his own, but kill? No—at least not Janet. Her death involved someone very powerful."

Jaxson held up a hand. "I trust your instincts."

I picked up Iggy, and together the three of us went back to my place. "I think this is the most stumped I've ever been on a case."

"Something will lead us in the right direction. It always does," Jaxson said.

"I hope so. I wonder if Mom or Gertrude can contact Janet? Being a witch, I would think she'd know what happened to her." To date, we had, at most, a fifty-percent success rate of the victim even appearing when asked, and only a small percent of those knew anything about their death. Usually, they merely had a feeling that something had gone wrong. "I've often wondered if the person is even aware they died?"

"Maybe not, but it doesn't hurt to ask," he said.

"True. Tomorrow, before and after my scene, I plan to pay closer attention to everyone, including the cameramen and the extras. I'm convinced Janet's killer is someone who works for Pink Moon Rising Productions."

"I bet you are right."

My alarm went off way too early the next morning, but for a change, I didn't mind. I had a lot to accomplish, and I wasn't talking about my acting gig. I needed to investigate.

I cleaned up in record time and then met Rihanna at the office. Iggy went over with me since he said he wanted to help Jaxson with the research. My little man knew nothing about computers, so I'm not sure what he could do, but I was game. Most likely, Iggy wanted to be in the office in case Hugo or Bandit showed up.

"Ready to spy?" I asked my cousin.

"Let's do this."

Together, we headed across the street. We were going to reshoot a scene with Lynn Lurch, the new Alexa, and Samuel, while Bethany would be helping behind the diner counter.

Since I hadn't been given the script, I had no idea when in the movie Gloria would kill Alexa, or if Shawn would shoot the retake scenes in chronological order for a change. I also had no idea how Gloria was going to kill Alexa.

Because my role was that of an insignificant waitress, Olivia wasn't assigned to do my makeup. Apparently, I was talented enough to do my own. Whatever.

When we entered the set, the inside was buzzing with activity. Cameramen were positioning themselves out of view of the action, and the director and Chris were conferring in the corner. Shawn didn't even look up when Rihanna came in with her camera slung around her neck. I wouldn't be surprised if he didn't notice her at all. The hard part of this little operation would be to stand where Rihanna could take pictures and not be in the movie itself.

I leaned closer to her. "How about snapping a few photos? That should get the director's attention. If he doesn't notice you, he's more oblivious than I thought."

"Sure. No problem."

She lifted her camera and fiddled with the settings. While she took a few shots, I went over to Bethany. "I'm sorry you have to redo so many scenes."

"Thanks. I feel the sorriest for Samuel. Interacting with different actors takes a toll on you."

I had no idea. "Where's Lynn?"

Bethany shrugged and then looked around. "I don't know. She's always on time."

"How is it working with her?" I'm not sure why I asked, but I liked Lynn and hoped this transition to lead would be a boost to her career."

"I can tell you she is a far superior actress to Janet, so for me, it makes it easier."

That comment implied Bethany didn't care for Janet. "I'm glad you like her."

Bethany smiled. "I do."

"Glinda!" the director called.

I spun around. Next to him was Rihanna. I guess he was more observant than I gave him credit. "Excuse me. I'm being summoned." I hurried off to the corner. "Yes?"

"This young lady claims to be your cousin," he said.

"She is." I explained about her being in school and needing to do a photo project. "She won't publish any of the photos if that is what's worrying you."

He stared at me for a moment. "Fine, but if she gets in the way, she has to go."

"Just tell her where to stand, and you won't know she's there."

"Over there." Shawn pointed to the back. He then looked around. "Where is Lynn?" he demanded.

Before I could respond, my cell vibrated. I lifted a finger to excuse myself and then moved away from the unhappy director. The text message was from Steve that read: *Glinda. I could use your help. Now.*

Every inch of my body froze. I couldn't remember the last time he'd texted me. If he had, I don't think it had been to ask for my help. I walked over to Shawn. "Excuse me, but the sheriff just texted me. He needs my help. I don't imagine I'll be long."

He looked around. "Since our new Alexa isn't here yet, go, but have your phone on in case I need you."

"Of course. I'll run right back." The running part was a figure of speech.

I turned around and tried opening my mind to Rihanna so she could read it. I wanted her to stay here and continue taking pictures. I wasn't sure what

I was hoping she'd find, but she'd surprised me in the past.

When she nodded that she understood, I smiled and hurried out. I couldn't for the life of me figure out how I could help Steve, but it must involve magic. Why else would he consult me?

I rushed down the street and then pushed open the door to the sheriff's office. Pearl's lips were pressed together, which wasn't a good sign.

"He's in his office," she stated without me asking her anything.

I would have asked Pearl what was going on, but it might be better not to delay. I lightly knocked on his door and then went in. Both he and Nash were there. "Hey."

"Have a seat, Glinda."

Yikes. I almost felt like I was being called into the principal's office. "What's going on?"

"We had another *confession*." Steve put air quotes around the last word.

"Who confessed?"

"Lynn Lurch came in just like Samuel Lipstein, acting like a zombie and said she wanted to confess to killing Janet Wood."

"You have to be kidding. Who is doing this?"

Steve crossed his arms over his chest. "That is why I need your help. We seem to have some rogue witch or warlock on our hands. It's possible Lynn really did kill Janet Wood, but considering her confession matched Samuel Lipstein's almost to the letter, I think she was also hypnotized."

I whistled. "Where is she now?"

"I put her in the cell. I figure after a good night's sleep, she'll be yelling for us to release her."

"Poor Shawn. The movie might never be made if no one was willing to play Alexa."

He shook his head. "Don't worry. I think he'll have his actress back in no time. Would you mind telling him what happened? Or do you think I should do it?"

I had to think what would cause the least disruption. "I'll do it. If the cast sees you, it will cause too much of a stir. How else can I help?"

"I know you can't tell who has magic and who doesn't, but keep watch on the other cast and crew members. I hope someone slips up."

"Can do." I explained that Rihanna was there taking pictures. "We want to see if she can catch someone doing something they shouldn't. We do have a large contingent of people—and animals—who want to help. Give them an assignment if you need anything."

"I will. And thank you."

Since Steve seemed finished with me, I had the

unpleasant chore of telling our esteemed director that the shoot between Lynn and Samuel Lipstein would have to be delayed, and I wasn't looking forward to that conversation. If I were in charge, I might ask Chris Pena to rewrite the diner scene between Alexa and Dr. Maynard out of the movie. It seemed to be cursed.

CHAPTER FOURTEEN

"She what?" Shawn said. To say he wasn't pleased would be an understatement.

"Don't be too harsh on her. It's not Lynn's fault." I explained again that she probably had no idea that she'd signed a confession. "The wording was the same as what Samuel said."

"Were they in cahoots?" Chris asked.

"I don't know, but I'm thinking not." Even if I explained about spells and hypnosis—which I didn't know much about—he wouldn't believe me. "Our sheriff thinks someone manipulated them."

Shawn furrowed his brows. "Manipulated how? Did they drug both of them and then use the power of suggestion to get them to do the killer's bidding?"

For a layman, that was a rather good explanation. "Other than we don't believe any drugs were used, you are pretty much spot on—except for the killing part. It's possible that whoever is doing this believes that if enough people confess, it will muddy the water so much that this person won't be caught. Sad to say, it has some validity."

Shawn leaned back in his seat. "Will Lynn wake up tomorrow and claim she had no idea that she signed any confession, like Samuel did?"

The man caught on quicker than I expected. "We believe so."

"Okay. If that's the case, I'll spend the rest of the day shooting around her. I'll move on to a scene with Dr. Maynard and Gloria. Tomorrow, when she is cleared, we'll continue."

That was an easy solution. "Sounds good."

Shawn gathered the talent and explained they were moving to the other location. Some were excused, while Shawn's assistant, Chuck, was asked to arrange for transportation to the other set right after he alerted a few of the others they would be needed.

"Does Penny need to be here?" I asked.

Shawn scrolled through his tablet. "No."

"Thanks." I walked over to Rihanna and told her about the change in plans. "What do you want to do? Do you think you have enough shots for the day?"

"I think so. I'd like to go back and look through

what I have. It's not like we couldn't drive over to the studio a little later if need be."

My cousin was a remarkable young lady. "I like it. Do you want to grab a drink at either the tea or coffee shop before we head back?"

"Sure, but you should call Jaxson. We don't want him to be upset that he's working while we're enjoying ourselves."

I smiled. "You are so right."

We decided on the tea shop for our snack. On the way, I called my hard working fiancé.

"You're finished already?" he asked.

"We didn't shoot anything because Steve texted me. Lynn Lurch confessed to killing Alexa, but we believe she was hypnotized just like Samuel."

"Seriously?"

"Yes. Rihanna and I are on our way to Maude's to have some tea. Want to join us?"

"I'd love to. See you in a few."

I debated suggesting Jaxson bring Iggy, because my familiar might decide to take off to find Bandit if Jaxson left him unsupervised, but I decided against it. I had to trust Iggy.

Rihanna and I snagged a table. When the server came over, I asked her to give us a minute since we were waiting for someone.

"I want to look through my shots," Rihanna said.

"Do you think you caught anything interesting?"

"No, but you never know when a photo comes in handy."

"You are so right," I said.

Two minutes later, the front door opened, and Jaxson breezed in. As soon as he spotted us, he smiled. What do you know? In the crux of his arm was Iggy.

"Someone wanted to join us," he said as he sat down.

"I thought you'd want to be with Bandit," I said.

"You guys usually know more."

I'm not sure that was true, but I'm glad Iggy wanted to join us. I nodded to the server that we were ready to order. As soon as Maude spotted Jaxson, she waved and rushed over.

"I heard that yummy actor confessed to killing his co-star, but then Steve let him go!" She pulled up a chair.

Maude had been the delivery system for gossip for a long time. It was time we returned the favor. "We believe he was hypnotized. Did you hear someone else confessed and said the same thing?"

Her eyes widened. "No. Pearl and I will have to have a little chat about her lack of communication."

If anything happened to the elderly lady, this town would find solving crimes really hard. "I think she's a little busy right now. I wouldn't be surprised if when Lynn wakes up, she doesn't remember a thing, just like Samuel."

"That is terrible. Do you know who might be hypnotizing them?"

"I wish." To give her a full rundown of what happened would take too long. "But don't worry, the three of us are on the case. We're sure real magic is involved as opposed to what a hypnotherapist could do."

Maude patted my arm and then smiled. "I know you'll figure it out. You always do. Now what can I get you all?"

We ordered, and I added my request for some lettuce for Iggy. He lifted one of his legs that made it look as if he was waving at her. The owner smiled and rushed off.

I turned to Jaxson. "Did you discover anything in the short time we were gone?"

"I did. I looked into Lynn Lurch's history. Apparently, she has been in quite a few films. Where she had a minor role, Janet was also cast."

"Interesting. Did you find that to be unique?"

"Unfortunately, no. It seems that when a director likes a person, he often requests that person for multiple movie roles."

Iggy crawled up Jaxson's arm, probably for a

better view. "Do you think this magic person is targeting medical people?" Iggy asked. "Maybe the doctor goofed and killed someone they loved."

What was he talking about? "Iggy, Samuel Lipstein is only playing a doctor. He isn't one in real life. Same goes for Lynn. She's only pretending to be a nurse."

"Oh."

Poor Iggy. I turned to Jaxson. "Any other interesting tidbits?"

"I think so. I found a photo of who I believe is Benson McDaniels."

He pulled a piece of paper from his pocket. The image wasn't the best, but it showed a thirty-something year old man with a beard and glasses. He was rather ordinary looking, which would make it hard to spot him in a crowd. "Rihanna, take a look. Maybe the guy is here already."

She studied the paper, but didn't say anything for a bit. "He actually looks familiar. Hold on."

Rihanna flipped through the pictures on her camera. Her lips pulled back and then pressed together. "He kind of looks like this guy, but kind of not."

Rihanna handed me the camera. I scooted my chair over to show Jaxson. I didn't think it looked like

Benson McDaniels, but it could be. "The guy in your photo looks older."

"I agree," Jaxson said.

"Could he be a relative?" Rihanna asked.

"I suppose he could. Let's pretend he is some relative of Benson's. Would he give his real name to the movie studio?"

"I don't know." Rihanna smiled. "But I have an idea."

"What's that?"

"People who aren't the main stars in a production seem to be invisible. How about I take pictures tomorrow, but I make sure to take a few extra ones of this guy? Maybe I'll even flirt with him a little."

"Rihanna!" She'd be acting, but I didn't want her to put herself in that kind of danger.

"What? It wouldn't be for real. I have Gavin, remember?"

"Of course, I do." I adored her boyfriend. Jaxson placed his hand on my arm as a signal to let him handle it.

"Rihanna, what if this guy is our killer? If he thinks you've figured him out, he might come after you," Jaxson said.

She nodded. "Fine, but I could ask him questions about lighting techniques. If he is a fraud, it will be easy to spot, even if I'm unable to read his mind. If he's not a killer, I'll learn some good information. Good photos are all about good lighting."

"Okay, but don't ask too many personal questions, or he might do something. What, I don't know." The idea of Rihanna snooping too much unsettled me.

"Ask Hugo to watch over you," Iggy said.

I looked over at him. "That is an excellent idea. Let's do that right after we eat."

Iggy lifted his head, clearly pleased with himself.

The next day, who should show up to the shoot but Lynn Lurch herself. She told everyone about the harrowing tale of confessing to killing Janet, but she remembered none of it.

"When I woke up this morning in the jail cell, I freaked. Thankfully, the sheriff was so nice and sympathetic. He said that someone must have hypnotized me."

The sleuth in me had to ask, "Lynn, who were you with before you walked to the sheriff's office?"

"No one. The last thing I remember, I was in my trailer. Next thing I know, I'm waking up in a freaking jail cell." She held up a hand. "If you mean before that, I was with Olivia since she had to do my makeup. Then I went back to my trailer since I had a few minutes before I had to be on the set. Then I woke up in the jail cell."

"That must have been so scary being in a strange place." Asking her any more questions in front of the crew would look a bit suspicious, so I stopped talking. I couldn't help but wonder, though, if Olivia had hypnotized her while applying her makeup. And did Olivia have anything to do with Samuel Lipstein's confession too?

Out of the corner of my eye, I spotted Rihanna cozying up to the lighting guy—aka the possible relative to Benson McDaniels. I wasn't all that hopeful that he was related to the man who had his script stolen, but I didn't want to judge before I was sure.

"Glinda, chop, chop," the director called. "You're up."

Sheesh. I painted on a smile and rushed over to Gloria and Dr. Maynard, since Gloria had, in theory, just finished her shift. I asked what they both wanted to eat and then headed to the kitchen to deliver my ticket to the imaginary chef. I hoped that Dolly had been informed that she needed to continue delivering the food. When I entered what was our *kitchen*, I found two plates of meatloaf that looked really good.

Since I needed to wait a few minutes before delivering the food, I came out of the back room and watched the camera crew focus in on the two actors at the table. Alexa entered from the front, and the moment she spotted the good doctor, she seemed to be totally infatuated with him. Since her role was to fall in love with him, I'd say she was a good actress. Better than Janet Wood in fact.

I had one more quick scene where I refilled their coffee before delivering their meal. Rihanna had been highly engaged with the lighting man until he had to start working. She then moved out of the way.

Once I placed their food in front of the couple, I stepped next to Rihanna and leaned close to her. "I'm done. Do you need to stay?"

My cousin shook her head. Together, we headed out through the back to the alley. If Hugo truly was watching her, he'd have exited with us. I glanced around but didn't spot anyone.

"Hugo, are you here? If you are, you can show yourself." He instantly appeared next to us. "Thanks for being our bodyguard."

He held up his palms. I guess that was to say it was his pleasure, or else it was ask if we needed him for further surveillance. It was hard to tell with Hugo.

I turned to Rihanna. "Was the lighting guy related to our screenwriter?"

"Maybe, but Hank—the lighting guy—was rather closed off. I couldn't get a good read on him. I sensed he was blocking me."

"Did you find out where he was from at least?"

"No."

"Hugo, can you follow him around? Hank might call someone after the shoot, Hopefully, it will be to Benson McDaniel." Trust me, that was wishful thinking on my part.

He nodded and then disappeared. "I'm going to see Steve," I told Rihanna. "Do you have time to go with me?"

"Sure. Are you wanting to get the inside info on Lynn Lurch and why she was released?"

"I can guess what she told Steve and why he had to let her go. No, I was hoping that Steve could find out more about Benson McDaniels and Hank the cameraman. Steve might learn enough to help Jaxson get the dirt on both of them."

Rihanna pressed her lips together. "You don't think Hank could kill anyone, do you?"

"I actually think he might have. To keep his cover intact, he'll finish the gig here, though."

"I didn't overhear anything in his mind to indicate that he's guilty. Actually, I didn't hear much, but my gut instinct tells me he's not a killer."

"I've had plenty of gut instincts. Some worked out, while others were total fails. Let's see if Steve can help."

CHAPTER FIFTEEN

"You think one of the lighting guys might be related to Benson McDaniels because he sort of looks like the guy who made a movie short?" Steve asked.

"Maybe. It's possible." Sheesh. He didn't have to sound so incredulous.

"And if he is, why do you think Benson's relative could be a killer?" Steve dipped his chin.

"Hey, it's always those you don't suspect who are often guilty," I said.

Steve held up a hand. "At this point in the case, I'm open to anything. I've never seen anything so crazy as people pouring in here and confessing to a crime they probably didn't commit."

"Witchcraft can mess with a person's head," I said.

"No kidding. As for Benson McDaniels, let me

see what I can find out about him and his family. The director is from New York, but I have no idea where this movie maker is from, but I'll have a chat with Mr. Shields. I bet he knows. He was very forthcoming when he admitted that he stole the short from McDaniels." Steve jotted something on his yellow note pad. "Do we know if Shawn has met him in person?"

I shook my head. "I wouldn't be surprised if he has though, which might be why his possible relative is here instead of Benson." I held up a palm. "That being said, it is possible I'm imagining this lighting guy is related, because I'm stumped as to who might be guilty."

"Let's say this guy... What's his name?"

"Hank," Rihanna said. "He never mentioned his last name, but he said he had a brother who was into cinematography. I didn't want to push too hard on that topic."

"Smart. If this guy is a powerful warlock, we don't need you being caught in his crosshairs, young lady. You best stay away from him until we know who he is."

I leaned forward. "Just so you know, I asked Hugo to watch over Rihanna. He's with Hank right now. I'm thinking after work, Hank might call someone, and if he does, Hugo will report back—via a translator, of course."

Steve's eyebrows rose. It seemed as if I'd impressed him. "That someone being this Benson McDaniel?"

"Sure. Why not?"

"Good thinking. Any other plans in the works I should know about?"

I glanced over at Rihanna. "Not at the moment. Jaxson is cross-checking who has acted together in other movies or television shows. Specifically, it would be good to know who worked with Janet Wood. It might provide us with a motive we hadn't thought of."

"I like that angle. I'll check out this lighting guy and get back to you. And smart thinking to have our gargoyle shifter act as Rihanna's bodyguard."

I nodded and then stood. "Let us know if you find out anything. This person of magic is still out there. I can't even guess if he or she will strike again."

"I will if I can."

Rihanna and I left. While I could use some lunch, I wanted to see if Jaxson had learned anything first.

When we entered the office, he and our two familiars were there.

Jaxson swiveled around in his chair. "Learn anything?"

Rihanna plopped down on the sofa, and Iggy came over and crawled onto her lap. "Just that Hank, the lighting guy, is good at blocking his thoughts. He appears to be outgoing, but he's definitely hiding something. He has a brother who is into movies, but that's all I learned," Rihanna said.

"Do you know where he's from?" Jaxson asked.

"No, but when we spoke with Steve, he said he'd find out from the director."

"Sounds good," Jaxson said. "Now what?"

I turned to Bandit. "You've been quiet. Did you learn anything?"

"Got anything to eat?"

I guess he only delivered if I fed him. "I haven't been to the store yet, but I will. I promise."

"Okay." He moved closer to the coffee table. I had the sense he liked being near Iggy. "I heard a lot of noise coming from Janet's trailer a little while ago."

"You mean the trailer that is now assigned to Lynn?"

"Yes, of course that's what I mean. It's not like a ghost needs that much space."

Snarky much? "What kind of noise?"

"I didn't have Hugo to teleport me inside, so the best I could do was climb up the side and look in. I kept slipping down the siding, so I didn't see much, but Lynn was searching in drawers and stuff."

My head ran in ten different directions. "Do you think we've been looking at this all wrong?" I wasn't addressing my comment to anyone.

"What do you mean?" Rihanna asked.

"Once more, I have no basis for this, but what if Lynn killed Janet in order to gain access to her trailer?" It sounded lame when I said it out loud.

"Are you thinking there is something in there that could incriminate Lynn?" Jaxson asked. "Or could she be looking for the evidence that proves Shawn stole Benson McDaniels' movie?"

"If she is looking for proof against Shawn, then she must not be aware that we already know about our director's shady past," I said.

"I'm thinking she's searching for something else. But what, we don't know," Rihanna said.

Iggy turned around on her lap. "You need to let me, and maybe Ruby, do a search, just like we did the last time when we were trying to find those stolen rubies."

"If you're hoping we will do another spell to allow you to move through a solid object, I don't know if it would work again."

"You can try," Iggy said.

"We have no idea what the long-term effect could have on your health. I won't chance it." Unless it was a matter of life and death.

Iggy tilted his head. "Are you making that up? I know you do that a lot when you don't want me to do something."

He knew that? I needed to watch what I said from now on. "It's my right to worry about you. But... I'm not against Genevieve taking you and Bandit inside the trailer during the day when Lynn is at work. However, you'll need to make certain to leave the place exactly as you found it. We don't want Lynn suspecting anything if she is guilty of murder."

He spun around. "Cool beans. When can we go?"

I hope this was smart to allow this. "I don't know Lynn's schedule. She might be in her trailer now."

"Hugo can go look," Iggy said.

"Maybe."

"Glinda, even if you find something, it won't be admissible in court," Jaxson reminded me.

I twisted toward him. "If Lynn Lurch is our killer —which I doubt—but if she is, then she won't be going to a regular prison anyway." Our *special* friends were tried in a magical court. I still didn't know how they prevented all the magic from occurring, but somehow they did.

"Good point. I guess you all will be wanting to go over to the Hex and Bones in order to ask for Genevieve's help?" he asked.

I glanced over at Bandit. I wasn't sure it wouldn't

be a bit suspicious if we went over there together. The shop was next to the studio set. "Let me call Andorra. It might be better if Genevieve came here."

"What about Hugo?" Iggy asked.

"He's watching one of our other suspects."

"Oh, yeah. I forgot."

I called Andorra and asked if she wouldn't mind sending over Genevieve. "We have a job for her."

"I'll ask her."

As soon as Andorra disconnected, our gargoyle shifter appeared. "You need me to do some more spying?" she asked with a smile.

I loved how excited she always was when we needed her. "Yes. This is a long shot, but Bandit heard the actress Lynn Lurch—the new Alexa—make quite a lot of noise in Janet Wood's trailer. He peeked in for a bit and saw her searching through drawers and such. It's possible—and this is a stretch—that she killed Janet to gain access to this trailer. Why? We don't know."

Genevieve's eyes widened. "I'm game, but I think you'll have better luck with Benson McDaniels' brother."

"What? How do you know Hank is Benson's brother?" I asked.

She smiled. "Whoops. I know Hugo wanted to be the one to break the news to you, but he's still with

Hank. Hugo wants to be certain he gets all the goods on the guy before he makes his full report."

All the goods? Genevieve must be watching quite a lot of television if she picked up that level of slang.

"Are you saying that Hank killed Janet?" Rihanna asked.

She shrugged. "I don't know why he would. He should be trying to harm the director to get back at him for what he did to his brother."

"Hank might not have had the opportunity. Come to think of it, I don't ever recall seeing Shawn without Chris," I said.

"Chris?" she asked.

"Chris wrote the screenplay that the movie is based on. I think they might be a couple, but I have no proof of that."

"I'll keep that in mind. So, what exactly do you need me to do?"

I explained how Iggy—who can no longer pass through wood—and Bandit wanted to help search the trailer. "We thought you could teleport them inside and help them look. I know Bandit can open drawers, but there might be places where even he can't reach."

"Sure. Now?"

"Since I believe Lynn is working—or at least I hope she was still filming—now might be a good time." I held up a hand, hoping she wouldn't disappear before I had the chance to explain. "She's probably not in her trailer, but check it out first. Be aware that she could return at any moment. If you hear anything, get these two out of there."

Genevieve planted a hand on her hip and rolled her eyes. "This isn't my first rodeo, girlfriend."

I laughed out loud. For someone who used to be a cement statue, she certainly had developed a great sense of humor. "You are right. I wish I could tell you what we are looking for, but I don't even know. Janet Wood is already dead, so I don't think Lynn would be looking for something to incriminate her."

"We'll check it out but don't discount that lightning guy until Hugo reports back."

"You mean lighting guy—not lightning."

She waved a hand. "You know what I mean." Genevieve turned to Iggy and Bandit. "Ready, boys?"

They both nodded. A second later, all three were gone. "Any guesses what they will find?" I asked.

Both Jaxson and Rihanna shook their heads.

My cousin stood. "I want to see if we've narrowed down our suspects at all."

"Good idea, but the issue can't be resolved until we know who has magic."

"I know, but we have to try," she said.

Rihanna carried over the board, and then Jaxson

joined us. When my cousin handed me the pen, I shook my head. "You lead."

"I've barely spoken to any of them."

"All the better to do this. I want you to be on your toes if you are with them," I said.

"Fine. Let's start with Hank. If Hugo is correct, he is Benson's brother. In that case, he definitely has a motive to harm Shawn, but I'm still not convinced he would murder Janet."

I made a motion with my hand for her to make a note of that. "Who's next?" I asked.

"Bethany Aldrich. We know she is a witch, and if she felt threatened that Janet might steal away the man she cares for, that is a good motive for murder."

"I agree. In fact, she might be my number one choice," I said.

"I thought you liked Lynn Lurch for it since she wanted the role Janet had."

I turned to him. I'd liked a lot of different people for Janet's murder at one time or another. "How did you know Lynn wanted the role? I know she was the understudy, but that doesn't mean she'd harm someone to get it."

"When I was looking at who had worked with Janet Wood, I learned that Lynn had competed for the same role as Janet three times and lost to her each time. If the reviewers are correct, Janet wasn't all that talented. The part should have been Lynn's, but for some reason, it went to Janet."

I leaned back against the sofa. "I'm thinking we need to talk with Shawn. He might know the real story."

"What real story?" he asked.

"You know my mind goes to the darkest place. I'm wondering if Janet Wood blackmailed him into taking her instead of Lynn even before this stolen movie issue."

"Call Steve," Jaxson said. "He might know."

"Good idea, and I will, but let's continue with our list. I know we eliminated Samuel Lipstein because he was hypnotized, but maybe we should put him back on the list."

"Why?" Jaxson asked.

"He could have faked it. I know that is a stretch, but I'm desperate."

After Rihanna added back his name, she tossed the pen onto the coffee table. "We have too many suspects. There has to be a way to narrow it down again."

"We can try contacting Janet Wood in the hereafter. It's been a few days. She might be willing to appear."

Jaxson checked his watch. "How about we see what Genevieve and Hugo uncover first?"

I didn't know why he was reluctant. Our séances had been successful in the past. I was fully aware that whenever the dead talked to us from the afterlife, the information was not always accurate. "Sure. Let's see what they have to say."

As if Jaxson was psychic, Hugo and Andorra popped up in the middle of our room.

"Sorry, guys." Andorra faced Hugo. "Please warn me when you're going to teleport me."

He nodded and then looked away.

"Genevieve was just here and said that Hugo learned a few things about Hank," Rihanna said.

I patted the seat next to me. "Andorra, come sit and relax."

Hugo, of course, remained standing. I think he was more comfortable that way.

"Hugo has learned a lot," Andorra told us. "He can confirm that Hank and Benson are brothers, but you won't believe why Hank is here."

CHAPTER SIXTEEN

EXCITEMENT RACED THROUGH ME. "Let me guess. He was sent to kill Shawn, but he wasn't able to find him alone, so he killed Janet instead?"

I swear Hugo cracked a smile.

"Nope. Quite the opposite."

I hadn't expected that answer. "Do tell."

"According to Hugo, when Benson McDaniels learned that the movie director had stolen his movie short, he threatened to go to the police."

"That could ruin a career pretty fast," I said.

"Exactly. To avoid that scenario, Shawn Shields offered to buy the rights to the movie."

I wonder why Shawn hadn't mentioned that to Steve. I could see where this was headed. "But Benson said no."

"Actually, he said no to the purchase, but he agreed to receive a share of the profits of *No Love Potion Needed* instead."

"I didn't see that coming," I said.

"Then why is Hank here if he isn't planning on harming anyone?" Rihanna asked.

Andorra consulted with Hugo and then faced us. "Benson was able to negotiate one more condition in the deal. His brother, Hank, has always been interested in movies, but he lacked experience."

I lifted a finger. "So Shawn had to hire Hank as well as give Benson a cut of the movie proceeds in exchange for the promise of Benson not going to the police."

"Exactly."

I mentally pumped a fist. "Hugo, what did Hank and Benson talk about on the phone?" I asked.

Andorra conferred once more. "They just talked about how the movie was going. After all, Benson stands to make a nice chunk of change if it's successful. Hank is partly here to make sure nothing goes wrong and partly to gain experience in being a lighting technician."

I huffed out a laugh. "I wonder what was going through either of their heads when the movie had to be recast thanks to Janet's murder?"

"Nothing good, I'm sure," Andorra said. "Have you figured out who might be responsible for her death?"

"No. We're just listing the potential suspects now, but we don't know who is and who isn't a person of magic—except for Bethany. The big problem we face is that many cast and crew members had a motive to kill Janet Wood, but who had the ability to do so is the big question."

"So now what?" Andorra asked.

Before I could answer, Genevieve and our two familiars returned from searching Lynn's trailer.

"Hugo!" Iggy shouted.

Hugo picked him up and placed him on his shoulder. I was happy to see those two were still friends. If they had ever argued, all seemed forgiven now.

"What did you find out?" I asked.

Jaxson dragged over another chair and motioned for Genevieve to sit down. "Thanks. We found two photos of Lynn Lurch with two different men. Shall we say, they were the type of photos she wouldn't want anyone else to see, if you know what I mean," she said.

"Can I see them? Pretty please? I won't tell," Iggy begged. "I don't care if Bandit thinks I'm not old enough. I am."

Genevieve must have decided Iggy shouldn't view them, and I figured she might be right. "Maybe later. Where did you find them?" I asked Genevieve.

"Actually Bandit located them. They were stuck underneath her desk—or what she used for a desk."

"Why would Janet have pictures of Lynn in what I can guess were compromising positions?"

"I don't know," Genevieve said.

"We believe that Janet Wood was blackmailing Shawn over his movie theft. Maybe she threatened to expose Lynn for what she had done too," I said.

"Other than enjoying herself, what was she really doing? It didn't look illegal to me," Genevieve said.

"I guess it depends on who these men were," I shot back. "I bet Steve can scan in the photos and run them through facial recognition software."

"That only works if they have a criminal record," he said.

I sorted through a few possibilities. "You're right. But if Lynn was involved, I'm thinking these men might be directors, producers, or leading men."

Genevieve shook her head. "I'd go with the first two. These guys weren't leading men types. Too old and too..."

How would she know? Genevieve spent most of her life as a gargoyle. Besides, I could think of a lot of older men who still got leading men roles. "I get it. I bet Shawn would know them, though."

"I have an idea," Jaxson said. "Let me scan in the photo, do a little Photoshop and crop out everything but the men's faces. If Shawn can't tell what the men are doing, he might be willing to tell us their names."

"I like it."

"Glinda, I take it you're thinking that Lynn is behind Janet's murder? Or do you think both Shawn and Lynn were in it together to kill Janet?" Jaxson asked. "That's assuming Janet was blackmailing both of them, of course."

"I don't know what to think. I could come up with ten scenarios proving that any number of people could have done in Janet Wood, but without knowing who possesses magic, we have nothing to go on."

"What can we do to help?" Genevieve asked.

"Keep an eye on Lynn?"

"Absolutely. Hugo and I are on it." She instantly disappeared.

"I love how she can do that," I said.

Jaxson laughed. "I'm glad you're finally getting used to her antics."

"She and Hugo are proving to be very valuable sleuths. We should make them honorary members of our company."

Jaxson grinned. "No telling what Genevieve would do if you did that."

"True." She was rather unpredictable. "I'm going to text Steve to let him know that Hugo discovered that Hank is Benson's brother, but that he came to learn and observe, not to kill."

"I'm sure he'll appreciate knowing that."

I wrote my text, read it over, and then sent it. "I guess there is nothing else we can do but wait until something else happens. I'm hoping our gargoyle sleuths can learn something new."

"Let's hope."

"I know it's a bit early for dinner, but I would like something to eat. Who's up for it?"

"I'll pass. I'm going to do some work and call Gavin," Rihanna said.

"You know I'm always game," Jaxson said.

I looked over at Iggy and Bandit. "What will you two do?"

Bandit glanced over at Iggy. "I know Hugo and Genevieve are working the Lynn angle, but I want to see about that makeup girl. She's cute," Bandit said.

I laughed. "I think she's a little out of your league. No offense. Besides, you can't hang out in the Magic Wand Hotel, you know?"

Iggy stepped over next to his new friend. "Ah, did you forgot he can cloak himself?"

"Olivia might remain in her room for hours."

Bandit lifted a paw. "We'll find a way to snoop. Maybe we'll see what Bethany and Samuel are up to then."

I smiled. "You do that."

I did not expect the tap on the face from Iggy in the middle of the night. When I roused, sirens were blaring down the road. "What's going on? Is the bookstore on fire?" My mind cleared. No, of course not. The bookstore burned down a while ago and now Courtney's Broomstick and Gumdrops shop sat in its place. I sat up. "Tell me."

"One of the trailers caught fire, and Hugo and Genevieve were there to save the day," Iggy said.

He wasn't making a lot of sense, so I threw off my covers and strode over to the window. I couldn't see the park very well since the strip mall was across the street and blocked the view, but I spotted smoke and several fire trucks. "When did you learn this?" I asked.

"Genevieve is in the living room. Ask her yourself."

"What? Now you tell me? Sheesh. Go tell her I'll be right out."

While he did that, I tossed on some clothes, quickly brushed my hair, and pulled it back into a ponytail. After slipping on my sneakers, I rushed out. I hadn't even glanced at the time, but by the total blackness outside, it was in the middle of the night. "Genevieve."

She raised an arm in apparent victory. "We got her."

"Who are you talking about?"

"Lynn Lurch. She's a witch, and I think she killed Janet."

I reached out to grab the back of the chair and then sat down. "Tell me everything."

She inhaled and then blew out a long breath. "You asked that we watch Lynn Lurch and her trailer."

"I remember."

"About a half an hour ago, Hugo spotted her leaving the hotel and going behind her trailer."

"She was outside in the middle of the night?" I asked.

"Yes."

"What was she doing there?"

Iggy crawled over. "How about letting Genevieve just tell you? Stop interrupting."

Really? I wasn't interrupting; I was clarifying, but I wasn't totally awake yet, so I might not be the best judge. "Sorry. Go on, Genevieve."

"Hugo thought it strange that she'd be outside, especially at that time, so he watched her put her hands on the back of the trailer, and a few seconds later, flames shot up inside."

"What? She set her own trailer on fire? Sorry. You're still telling us what happened."

Iggy shook his head while Genevieve smiled. "That's okay. Once Lynn had performed her magic, she stepped back and took out her phone." Genevieve pulled out her cell. "Hugo used my phone to record her call. Since he was cloaked—as was the phone—he placed it as close to Lynn's as possible so it would record both sides of the conversation."

I wanted to ask who Lynn called at in the middle of the night, but I'm sure I'd find out if I just waited a bit. I nodded for her to play it for me.

"Crystal, it's me. I did it," Lynn said.

"You got Sam to fall in love with you?"

"Not yet, but there are no more pictures of me with any directors. No one can touch me now."

"Thank goodness Janet will no longer be in your way," Crystal said.

"No kidding. And the beauty of it all is that no one knows a thing. Look, I have to take off and seek comfort from Sam. He'll be so supportive now that my trailer is destroyed—or will be shortly. Bye."

"Love you."

It took all of my control not to comment after each sentence. "I'm blown away. Did Lynn just admit to killing Janet?"

"She didn't come out and say it, but the fact that no one knows a thing kind of implies it," Genevieve said.

This evidence might not be legal in a regular court, but since Hugo had seen Lynn set the trailer on fire, it would prove she is a witch. Knowing who killed Janet might help Steve find some needed evidence.

"Who called the fire department?" I asked.

Genevieve glanced upward. "I did, but don't worry, the trailer has little damage."

"I thought you said she set it on fire."

"I bet Hugo put it out," Iggy piped up.

"That's right. I forgot he could turn his hands to ice." How he put out the blaze with cold hands, I have no idea. "I'm going to call Jaxson and have him meet us in the park. It makes sense we'd run out there. The sirens probably woke up half the town."

"I'm going with you," Iggy said.

"Absolutely. Do you know where Bandit is?"

Genevieve answered. "He's with Hugo. They'll make sure Lynn doesn't try to escape."

I doubt she would since she'd be certain no one would suspect her. I imagine no accelerant was used

—just magic hands. I pulled out my phone and called Jaxson. While he was a little groggy, he seemed to understand what happened. "Can you meet us in the park?"

"I'm happy to, but what good will it do?"

"I don't know. I'm just curious. We'll need to tell Steve what happened."

I swear I could see him smile. "I'm sure he knows already, but I'll meet you there."

Once I gathered my jacket and my familiar, we headed over there. Genevieve said she'd travel her own way.

No surprise, we could only get as close as the sidewalk. The fire department had taped off much of the remaining area. Thankfully, the park had lights. "Iggy, you have good eyesight. Is that Lynn with Samuel Lipstein?"

"Put me down, and I'll move closer."

I placed him on the grass. "Don't let anyone see you."

One second he was there, and the next he wasn't. I imagine Hugo was standing next to the lovebirds, so I had no fear anything would happen to my familiar.

Steve and Nash both showed up and hightailed it over to Ian Silver, the arson investigator. I couldn't imagine always having to be on call like that.

Those two lawmen were so focused on their job

that neither seemed to notice me. Less than fifteen minutes later, Jaxson arrived.

"Any news?" he asked.

CHAPTER SEVENTEEN

"No, but Iggy is over by Samuel's trailer. I think he's with Lynn. He'll get the scoop," I said.

"No fire hoses?" Jaxson asked.

"Hugo put the fire out. I need to ask more questions, but I think Lynn assumed that once the blaze started, it would continue. From what I can remember about the timing, once she made a phone call to someone named Crystal, she ran off to find Samuel, her true love."

"You're saying the fire was set partially to get Samuel to offer her comfort?" Jaxson asked.

I shrugged. "I'll need to listen to the phone conversation again, but I think so."

"You said Genevieve has the phone recording?" he asked.

"She does. I hope she hands it over to Steve."

Steve walked over to Lynn while Nash continued conversing with Ian Silver. A fireman came out of the trailer. Since he wasn't rushing out, it confirmed what Hugo said—the place wasn't on fire. I'd have to remember to tell Steve to have the men look for a palm print on the outside of the trailer. Whether anyone would believe a person had such powerful hands, I didn't know, but that was what happened.

Small feet pressed on my leg, and a second later, Iggy was in full view. "What did you learn?"

"It's sickening."

"What do you mean?"

"Lynn was all weepy, saying that everything she had was destroyed. Can't she see there wasn't much damage?" Iggy said.

"Maybe. I say we go back to bed and talk with Steve and Nash tomorrow. Did you see Bandit?"

"If he was invisible, how could I see him?"

That was a good question, and if Lynn was a witch, Iggy couldn't call out. "I don't know." I turned to Jaxson. "Sorry to drag you out. There's really nothing to see."

"I'm glad you called. How about I stop by your place tomorrow, say about ten? We can eat and head on over to the sheriff's department. Or do you have to shoot a scene?"

"With the fire and Lynn's sort of confession, I'd

completely forgotten about the movie. I'll have to look at my calendar, but I don't think I'm needed tomorrow."

Jaxson walked us back to my place, kissed me goodnight, and left. The moment I hit the sack, I fell asleep, which was unusual when we were dealing with a crime.

Turns out it wasn't my alarm that woke me up but rather a call from Steve at nine. I patted my nightstand for my phone and answered. "Hello?"

"Glinda, I know it's early, but I have several people in the conference room who have asked that you join them. I hear someone more or less confessed to murder."

I smiled. How awesome that the sheriff called me. "Yes. Give me a few, and I'll be right over."

"And bring Iggy. I heard he was involved in this whole affair too."

"What about Bandit?"

"He's here with Hugo," Steve said.

Whoa. "I'll call Jaxson."

Then I hung up before he could tell me his presence wasn't needed. I contacted Jaxson and told him that Steve had requested our presence.

"That explains the early phone call," he said.

"Yes. Obviously, I'll have to take a rain check on breakfast until later."

He chuckled. "I'm already at the office, but Rihanna left for school. I know she'll be disappointed that she missed this."

"For sure. Meet you at Steve's office."

Needless to say, Iggy and I were the last to arrive. I was surprised to see Shawn Shields and Chris Pena in the conference room with our gargoyle shifters, Jaxson, and yes, Bandit.

I wonder how Steve was so certain the director and the writer weren't involved? Of all the initial suspects, Shawn had the most motive to want Janet Wood dead. I guess it was his apparent lack of magic that convinced Steve of the man's innocence.

I went into the room and sat next to Jaxson.

"Good," Steve said, "we can begin. I had Genevieve play the recording of Lynn's conversation. While highly interesting, it's not conclusive that she is the killer."

"What about the video that Hugo took?" Genevieve asked.

"What video?"

Had she only shared the voice recording? I looked over at her and raised my eyebrows.

"Whoops. Sorry. I forgot about that." Genevieve

showed him her phone and Steve played the recording. "It shows Lynn placing her hands on the back of the trailer and then the insides catch on fire."

"How did she do that?" Steve asked.

"How does Hugo turn his hands to ice? It's magic," Genevieve said.

"I see."

I wish I knew more about how she did it. "Clearly she has powerful hands, but the big question is whether they are powerful enough to kill a person?"

"That's what we need to find out," Steve said. "Once I heard what Hugo witnessed, I asked Nash to fingerprint the back of the trailer. There were two palm prints there all right. While we could arrest her for arson, no court would believe it."

Both Shawn and Chris shook their heads. Some people would never be believers. Trying to convince them that someone was able to basically do a brain drain on Janet wouldn't serve us right now either. "We need proof that Lynn killed Janet Wood."

"Tell us your great plan," Steve said. "You always have one."

"Not this time, but in the past we've done some kind of sting operation. However, I'm certainly not going to pretend to like Samuel—for many reasons— just to expose myself to Lynn's jealousy. We have to remember that she is a powerful witch. She is certainly no match for me."

"Can she teleport or cloak herself?" Iggy asked.

He was always comparing all people of magic against Hugo. "I don't know." I turned to Genevieve. "Last night, did Hugo see her do either of those things?"

Genevieve shook her head. "No. I asked him. And she would have become invisible if she were able. She had to believe that someone might have seen her near her trailer when it caught on fire."

"That's true," Nash said. "It doesn't look good for Lynn that she didn't call the fire department. Genevieve did. Since Lynn wasn't very careful, maybe we can use that to our advantage."

We could debate Lynn's lack of planning for hours, but the bottom line was that we needed more evidence that she was the killer—even in the court of magic.

"Steve, do you have those photos of Lynn with other men?"

"Yes. I showed them to Shawn, and he was able to identify both men as other directors—make that married directors. Lynn was in both of the movies these men directed."

"Good to know, but she was willing to burn a whole

trailer to eliminate those pictures?" I asked. "If she did kill Janet, was that the real motive? From her conversation with this Crystal person, Lynn wanted to gain sympathy from Samuel. " Lynn was a lot younger than Samuel Lipstein, but he was a big movie star, so maybe.

No one answered for a moment.

"From what you've indicated, Lynn was enamored with Samuel," Jaxson said, "but why not just kill Bethany? It seems as if he's given his heart to her, which would upset Lynn."

He had a point. "Bethany wasn't blackmailing her, Janet was—or so I'm assuming," I said. "Why else keep those pictures of Lynn?"

"True." Steve turned to Hugo. "Hey, buddy, can you be Bethany's bodyguard until we figure out a way to prove Lynn is guilty?"

Hugo nodded and then disappeared. I glanced out of the glass-enclosed conference room. No one was there, but both Chris and Shawn seemed to be in shock.

"What just happened?" Chris asked.

I wasn't going to touch that one. I tilted my head at Steve. Let him answer that.

"It's complicated," our sheriff said. "As I said, magic exists, and you just witnessed a small part of it."

Shawn stabbed a hand over his head. "I can see I need to be a bit more open-minded."

"I'm glad that Bethany will be safe," Chris said.

Genevieve raised her hand. Every time she did that, I cracked a smile.

Steve nodded to her. "Do you have an idea?"

"I do."

When she didn't elaborate, I figured Genevieve wanted to be asked. "What would that be?"

"Let me make Lynn Lurch jealous."

"No!" I blurted. "She'd kill you."

Genevieve leaned back in her seat and grinned. "Did you forget who I am?"

I don't think she wanted me to spell it out in front of these two men. "Are you saying she can't hurt you?"

"Ding, ding."

I had to laugh. "You've been watching too much television."

"I know. Isn't it wonderful?" She grinned.

"Genevieve, can you elaborate?" Steve asked. "How do you plan on accomplishing this? I trust you'll want Samuel Lipstein in on this plot to make Lynn jealous."

She looked over at me. I guess that meant she wasn't sure. "Shawn, you would know better," I said. "Do you think it is wise to let Samuel know that Lynn might be the killer? If he is aware of what she's done —or what we think she's done, he might react differently with her during the scenes."

"Samuel is an actor, and a good one at that. He can handle it." The director looked over at the screenwriter. "Chris what do you think?"

Chris bit down on his lip. "When were you planning on reshooting the scene where Alexa does the love spell on Dr. Maynard?"

"I'd have to look at my notes, but it's coming up soon."

That could spell disaster—no pun intended. "May I ask where you purchased the herbs and stuff for the spell Janet did?"

"I'd have to ask my assistant, but I think she said Lynn would take care of it herself. I know Janet did."

That wasn't what I wanted to hear. "Is there any way you can delay that scene for a bit? Be aware that she might put a real spell on Samuel when he's unaware—assuming she was the one who hypnotized him."

"Then who hypnotized Lynn?" Shawn asked.

"I'm thinking she was just acting. Steve, you said the two stories were almost the same, right?"

"Yes. It was like there was one script, which was why I thought she was telling the truth. In hindsight, the scripts were probably the same since she wrote it."

"I agree. How about a group of us brainstorm this? If it's okay with Shawn, don't say anything until the sheriff gives you the all clear," I suggested.

He blew out a breath. "This movie isn't going to be made, is it? If Lynn is guilty, who is going to take her place? That role seems to be cursed."

The image of Chris' sister came to mind. "You can use Chris' sister, Lisa, assuming she can handle the role. Or else, Chris can rewrite some of the scenes, eliminating the need to do the love spell. But I've not read the script. I just heard that's what happens."

Shawn nodded. "Chris and I will brainstorm ideas too. I can't thank you all enough for helping."

Those two left. Bandit and Iggy had been in the corner chatting away. Never once did Shawn or Chris even glance their way, confirming at least to me that neither had any magic.

"Why don't you guys come over to the store?" Genevieve asked us. "We can hash out the details."

"Great. I'll call in a To-Go order from the Tiki Hut. I'm starved."

"When aren't you hungry?" That snarky comment came from my darling iguana.

"I'm tempted to let you and Bandit stay here.

Steve can lock you two in so you can't cause any harm."

Bandit stood on his hind legs. "You wouldn't dare."

If I didn't think he could help, I just might do that. "You can come if you behave. We could use your help."

"Okay." He actually sounded cheerful.

We thanked Steve and Nash and headed out the front door. I was glad that Genevieve didn't try to teleport. While we walked down the street, I ordered food for me, Jaxson, and some extra sweets for Andorra, Elizabeth, or Bertha, in case they wanted to join us.

"What about food for me?" Bandit asked.

Sheesh. "Throw in a plate of tuna and any leftover food for the raccoon." Since I was chatting with my aunt, she'd know what I meant.

"I'll have it ready in a few minutes. Will you pick it up?" Aunt Fern asked.

I looked over at Jaxson. He must have heard her question through the phone since he nodded. "Yes."

With everything set, we went into the Hex and Bones. Luckily, all three ladies were working. I motioned Elizabeth and Andorra over to the counter while Bertha finished up with a customer.

"Any news on the trailer fire?" Andorra asked.

"Plenty." I was surprised that Hugo hadn't stopped in the store first and filled her in before fulfilling his bodyguard duties. "I'll tell you all about it, and then I'd like your help coming up with a plan to take down the arsonist, who most likely is the killer."

Andorra almost squealed. "My favorite thing to do.

CHAPTER EIGHTEEN

WE MOVED INTO THE BACKROOM. Bertha insisted that her granddaughters help with the case while she tended the store. I didn't know what was going to happen once Bertha retired. She was so knowledgeable with spells and could handle the store by herself if need be.

While I explained the events of last night and this morning to Andorra and Elizabeth, Jaxson went over to the Tiki Hut to pick up the food.

"Genevieve, why don't you tell them your idea about how to catch the killer?"

"Sure."

She was only halfway through her plan when Jaxson returned with our food along with some for the animals. We ate while Genevieve finished outlining her idea. I was impressed that she'd improved on it a bit.

"I like it, but what about Samuel?" Elizabeth asked. "You'll have to tell him, right? If he's in love with Bethany, as you claim, he won't be openly affectionate with Genevieve."

She was right. "I see no way around not telling him and Bethany," I said.

"What will you tell them though?" Jaxson asked. "Will you really say you suspect Lynn of murder?"

Andorra snapped her fingers. "No. We should only tell them that Lynn set her trailer on fire—even though she failed—in order to earn some sympathy from him. He might have a hard time being around her even with that, but we have to ask him to lead Lynn on. He'll have to rely on his acting skills. Lynn needs to believe she has a chance with Samuel. We certainly don't need her to become upset and kill him."

"That would be terrible," I said. "We should have Bethany throw a hissy fit in front of Lynn. That way Lynn will only see Genevieve as the rival, and not Bethany."

"Good thinking, Glinda. Even though Hugo is there to keep her safe, it would be best if Lynn only has her eyes on Genevieve," Jaxson said.

"Not to be a spoilsport, but how are we going to

introduce Genevieve onto the set without raising suspicion?" I asked.

"We could say she's an ex-girlfriend who learned that Samuel was in Florida," Andorra offered. "Maybe she lives in Tampa and decided to drive over here. As a backstory, maybe she dumped him right before he met Bethany, which is why we haven't seen her before. Genevieve might have realized that she'd made a mistake and wanted to get back with him."

We sat there for a bit trying to find the holes in that plan.

"I know what we should do," Bandit said.

This should be good. He had the most experience being on set so he might have a good suggestion. "What is that?"

"Everyone likes food, right?"

I had no idea what that had to do with anything. "Yes."

"Then have Genevieve deliver some baked goods to the set. If she's an old—I mean former—flame, she could think the way into his good graces would be to show him how hot she is now."

What? How did a raccoon know anything about what was good looking or not? It didn't matter. "That would imply they broke up a year or two ago to allow Genevieve to have time to improve her looks."

"I don't look good?" She stood up and posed.

She didn't get it. "Yes, you look amazing. This is what we tell the others. You came back to show your former boyfriend that he was a fool to let you walk away—or whatever happened between you two."

"Oh, okay," she said.

"Thoughts?" I asked.

"It sounds good. We could have Shawn buy the baked goods from both Maude's and Miriam's shop, and Genevieve could be the delivery person," Elizabeth said. "Your director could say that with all the upheaval of late, he wanted to give the cast something nice.

They did have the best baked goods in town. "I'm sure he'll agree. Now, we need to find out whether anyone has an objection to bringing Bethany and Samuel on board."

"I'll ask Steve," Genevieve said. "But don't worry, Glinda, I'll look before I leap." And then she was gone.

I sipped my tea and finished eating my breakfast, or rather my lunch. It wasn't more than a few minutes before Genevieve walked in with the sheriff.

"I hear you have a plan," he said.

Since Genevieve might have forgotten a few details, I outlined everything again. "I think I'll ask Rihanna to take pictures or video what's going on in case we need it in court—our court, not yours. I know that kind of evidence isn't admissible."

Steve's lips curled up for a moment. "Genevieve asked if we could tell the plan to Samuel and Bethany. I think it is absolutely necessary."

"Shawn, too, and by extension, Chris?" I asked.

"Them, too, but no one else, not that there are many left."

"Do you want to tell them?" I asked.

"I will contact Shawn and perhaps set up the delivery for tomorrow," Steve said. "We want this to look as seamless as possible."

"They'll want to meet Genevieve first," I said.

Steve took a moment. "Good idea, but let's not tell them she has any powers. We don't want to shock them too much."

Most of us laughed. "We definitely don't want to do that."

Steve stood. "I'll make the arrangements. Glinda, why don't you and Jaxson let Maude and Miriam know that we'll be needing some goodies starting tomorrow, and that Genevieve will be picking up, say, a box of sweets from each place."

I looked over at Genevieve. "Do you have a credit card?"

Steve held up a hand. "Tell her to put it on my tab. I'll have Shawn reimburse me."

"Sounds good."

He turned to Genevieve. "I'll see you tonight."

With the plan in place, I wanted to return to the office to see if Rihanna was back from her classes. She would play a role too.

"What should we do?" Bandit asked.

"The trailer did have some damage to the interior, but how about if you hide underneath and watch the interaction between Lynn, Samuel, and Bethany. If you see any tensions brewing, let me know."

"Aye, aye captain."

I cracked a smile. "Thanks."

"And me?" Iggy asked.

"You're coming with us. We'll need your brain power to make sure we haven't forgotten anything."

Iggy faced Bandit. "I told you she was like that— always making stuff up. She thinks I don't know what she's doing."

"Sorry, dude," Bandit said.

I'd had enough of these two. I lifted Iggy and placed him in my purse. "Let's go, Sherlock."

I was nervous. I was about to do another scene, this time with Alexa and Dr. Hottie. Steve had given Samuel and Bethany the rundown, but so far,

Samuel Lipstein was acting as if he harbored no ill feelings against his *co-star*. That impressed me to no end.

At this point in the movie, he hadn't had the love spell, so he didn't have to act all lovey-dovey with Lynn. I walked over to their table with a pot of coffee, and with more cheer than I felt, I poured them their drinks.

"Can I take your order?"

Nurse Alexa ran her finger down the fake menu. "I'll have a number seven."

Dr. Hottie ordered a number four. I pretended to scribble down the information and went into the back. Bethany rushed in from the alley entrance.

"The sheriff said they suspect Lynn of setting her trailer on fire?" She'd whispered it even though no one could hear us in the front.

"I heard that too."

"He also said you knew this Genevieve lady. She's on the up and up, right?"

I wasn't sure what that meant, but I think she wanted me to say yes. I was surprised Steve hadn't arranged for the two of them to meet beforehand. He said they both needed to know.

"Absolutely. She knows her role is to make Lynn jealous so she'll admit to setting her trailer on fire so that she could get close to Samuel."

Bethany shivered. "Thanks for telling us beforehand. I think this will be the role of a lifetime."

I smiled. "You'll do great."

"Gotta go. I'm up next."

"Good luck."

I came out of the back a few seconds after Bethany and walked over to another table. While I pretended to have a conversation with the occupants, I listened to Samuel and Lynn's conversation. To my delight, Samuel delivered his lines exactly the same way he had with Janet.

After only two takes, Shawn said he was happy with the scene. He probably realized that the scene would have to be shot again with yet another Alexa once this Alexa was arrested for arson and hopefully murder.

"Let's take five, people," Shawn said. "As a thank you for redoing these scenes, I've hired someone to deliver snacks. She should be here shortly."

Most likely Genevieve was already there. She would teleport out and then walk through the door like an ordinary human.

One minute later, she did just that. As soon as she stepped inside with her arms full of goodies, Samuel jumped up.

"Let me help you." Before he took hold of the goodies, he stilled. "Genevieve? Is that you?"

"It sure is. You going to help me or what?" She gave him a megawatt smile. All her television watching seemed to be paying off. She was a good actress.

Rihanna was off to the side, but we wanted to have as many shots of Lynn's reaction as possible. And we weren't disappointed. Lynn was giving Genevieve the evil eye.

Samuel and Genevieve stood there chatting rather loudly, and when he let out a laugh, Lynn pushed back her chair and went over to the seemingly happy couple.

The smile she'd painted on was clearly fake. She introduced herself as Samuel's costar. "And who are you?" she asked in a not very cordial voice.

I had to hand it to Genevieve. She and Samuel must have come up with a backstory that would hold up under scrutiny. She even played the southern belle quite well.

"My name is Genevieve Dubois. Samuel and I were...well...lovers. We broke up, but then I realized that I had made a terrible mistake not finding him right after we had our little spat. When I heard he was only an hour away from where I now live, I was ecstatic. I just had to see him."

Lynn ran her gaze up and down Genevieve. "So you got a job as a delivery girl just to see him?"

Uh-oh. I hope our gargoyle shifter was fast on her feet with answers. I supposed we should have had her wear an earpiece so that someone could have fed her answers.

"Why not? There are a ton of people who want to see my Sammy. This assured I'd have access." She ran a finger down his chest.

Meow! The claws were out tonight. Good job, Genevieve.

Shawn must have decided he needed to intervene. "Chop, chop, people. Let the young lady through. I'm in need of my sugar fix."

He showed Genevieve where to place the goodies. Because it was a little uncomfortable in the room, I rushed over to grab a snack.

Genevieve rubbed Samuel's arm. "I think we need to talk. Tonight? Your trailer? No one will disturb us there."

"Sure."

Genevieve smiled and sashayed out the door.

CHAPTER NINETEEN

BECAUSE IT APPEARED as if Lynn bought the whole former girlfriend angle, we thought it would be okay for Hugo to be around Samuel and Genevieve instead of watching Bethany Aldrich.

That job would go to Bandit. While he was no bodyguard, he could hurt someone who came near her. Since Bethany was a witch, she would be able to communicate with him.

It was two nights later, after the shoot, that Bethany had her angry scene with Samuel, telling him that he was paying too much attention to Genevieve. Jaxson, Rihanna, and I hid in the fake diner so we could watch. Bethany was wearing a wire so that Steve and Nash could hear in case they needed to intervene. We, however, couldn't hear anything, which totally frustrated me. However, the arm waving, and the way Bethany was leaning in toward Samuel, implied she wasn't happy with the man.

The smile on Lynn's face told me she bought the whole thing.

As soon as Bethany stomped off toward the hotel, Lynn grabbed Samuel's hand. He shook his head and then nodded to his trailer. Just then, the door opened, and who should appear, but Genevieve!

Lynn planted her hands on her hips and seemed to deliver a similar tirade at him. The poor man was being put through the ringer—and to think all but Lynn's reaction was fake.

"How about we head on over to the station—assuming Steve is watching from there?" I said.

"What more do you need to know?" Jaxson said.

"I don't know."

Rihanna placed a hand on my arm. "How about we see what happens tomorrow? Between Hugo, Genevieve, and Bandit, nothing will happen to Bethany or Samuel tonight."

She was right. "Sure, and since everything is being recorded, we'll have proof if Lynn tries anything."

The shake to my shoulder woke me. When I opened my eyes, I was still on my living room sofa with soft light streaming in the window. I clearly had fallen asleep.

I blinked a few times to clear my eyes. "Genevieve?"

"We got her."

"What do you mean you *got her*?"

Genevieve sat next to me on the sofa. "It's a long story. Do you want to call Jaxson? Steve already knows, but I thought I should tell you in person."

What she was saying wasn't really making sense, but I hadn't had my cup of coffee yet. "Sure."

I made the call. "Can you meet Genevieve and me at the office? She has news."

"Sure, but I'm already here."

"Has Rihanna left for school."

"No, she's still in her room."

I had to think. "I'll be right over. Make me some coffee, will you?"

He chuckled. "I'm on it."

I disconnected. "Give me a second to freshen up."

"I'll just go over to the office while you get ready." And then she was gone.

Iggy crawled off his stool and came over. "What do you think happened?"

"We'll find out in a minute."

I quickly cleaned up, picked up my little buddy, and rushed over to the office.

"Do you think Bandit is okay?" Iggy asked on the way there.

"I'm sure he is, or Genevieve would have said something. Besides, Hugo would never let anyone harm him."

"You're right."

Needing my coffee something fierce, I practically jogged up the office stairs. When I stepped inside, Jaxson picked up a steaming mug and handed it to me. He then leaned over and gave me a kiss.

"Thank you," I said.

"Sit down so we can begin."

Genevieve, Rihanna, Bandit, and Hugo were there. "Hi, everyone. Since you all look happy—or at least Genevieve does—I'm assuming all went well?" I asked.

I placed my bag on the coffee table so that Iggy could crawl out. No surprise Hugo stepped over and lifted him up, while Bandit remained by Hugo's side. The man was quite the pied piper of familiars.

I sipped my brew and let the rich taste wake me up. "Tell me what happened."

Genevieve stood in front of us, clearly enjoying being the center of attention. "Let me say that I took one for the team."

I cracked up. "Where are you learning these phrases?"

"I heard Andorra use it. Anyway, I had to make out with Samuel in front of Lynn." She leaned forward. "Just so you know, he's not a great kisser like someone else is."

Eww. "Too much information, but go on."

While Hugo was good looking, to say the least he was rather stiff. I couldn't imagine him kissing Genevieve, nor did I realize they had those kind of feelings for each other. After all, they'd spent most of their lives as slabs of cement.

"We only made out—as the teenagers would say— when Lynn was around. Since our goal was for Lynn to try to kill me, I sat out on the steps of the trailer."

"Without Samuel?" I wanted to make sure I understood.

"Yes. In less than five minutes, she came to *talk*— or at least that was what she said."

I looked over at Hugo. "Was your protector around?"

"Both of them were." She smiled at Bandit. "Poor Lynn will probably have a scar for life."

"This should be good. Tell me more."

"She asked me what my plans were, like did I intend to stay in Witch's Cove until the movie ended, and did I really think that Samuel actually cared for me. Blah, blah, blah. She was rather pathetic."

"Do you think she really loved him?" Rihanna asked.

"I'm no expert on love, but I think she wanted something she couldn't have. The woman seemed very driven to succeed. She might have thought that if she attached herself to a star that she could get better roles."

The fact she had affairs with several directors kind of backed up that theory. "What happened? Did she try to kill you?"

"I'm getting to that. Be patient." I held up a hand and motioned that she continue. "After Lynn told me that she was interested in Samuel, she said she was chilly and could we go to her trailer where she had something warmer to put on."

"Did you think she'd try to kill you?" I asked.

"Most definitely. I picked up Bandit and said that I'd adopted him so he needed to come with me." Genevieve looked over at him. "If I hadn't said something, she wouldn't have allowed him in her trailer with us. Anyway, Lynn told me all sorts of lies about how Samuel loved her and that he was leading me on. You get the gist. That's when she leaned over and placed her hands on the side of my head."

I sucked in a breath. "What did you feel?"

"Pain, but like I said, I'm not built like ordinary humans. I telepathed to Hugo to stay back. Having a woman place her hands on my head wouldn't stand up in court. Am I right?"

I smiled. "You've come a long way, Genevieve."

She grinned. "It's been so much fun being a human. Anyway, I wanted her to think she'd killed me, so I passed out. Since I am capable of being a statue, I could stop my heart."

That sounded scary and maybe dangerous, but since she stated it with such calmness, perhaps it wasn't. "Then what?"

"Three guesses."

What would I have done? "If she tried to get rid of the body, where would she take it to make it look like she wasn't involved?"

Rihanna sat up straighter. "No, she would have called 9-1-1. She'd pretend as if she had no idea what happened. She would cry and say this woman just passed out and died. Since Genevieve had no marks on her body, Lynn couldn't be accused of murder— even though Genevieve wasn't really dead."

The gargoyle smiled. "You win, Rihanna."

My cousin smiled and clapped.

"Did Steve come in then?" I asked.

"Actually, it was two guys with a gurney who arrived next. I think Steve told me afterward that they were from the morgue."

"When you were safely in the van, you teleported out of there, right?" I asked.

"I did not. That would have freaked out some people."

My mouth opened. I then clapped. "I am very proud of you for thinking that."

"So what happened?" Rihanna asked.

"Once at the morgue, I was delivered to that smelly room. As soon as Elissa came in, I sat up. She'd been told by Steve that I was faking my death."

"What about Bandit and Hugo?" I asked.

"Since Hugo was inside the trailer recording everything—in his cloaked form, of course—once Lynn went outside to watch the men load my body into the ambulance, Hugo took off with Bandit."

"She would have left him in there, I bet, trapped for who knows how long," I said.

"Probably."

"What did Steve do about Lynn?" Jaxson asked.

"Steve couldn't arrest her until after my *autopsy*, which was why he didn't arrest her—at least not then. He understood that she needed to be handled carefully."

"That may be, but I still don't see how this proves that Lynn killed Janet Wood even if she tried to kill you," I said.

She looked at Hugo and smiled. "Hugo has a

recording of what Lynn said over my dead body. She laughed and said now all the women in Samuel's life were gone—except for Bethany, who, by the way would be next."

"Then why isn't Lynn in custody?" She just threatened to kill Bethany!

"Actually, Steve called the place that handles powerful people of magic. They are on their way to arrest her."

I leaned back. "Wow. The man is a true believer."

"He is. It didn't hurt that Hugo placed his hands on the side of Lynn's head after he immobilized her and learned that she had killed Janet. We know that can't be used in the human court, and it might not be admissible in the magical court, but at least we know."

"Good job, Hugo." I returned my focus to Genevieve. "I thought you said that Bandit attacked Lynn."

"Oh, yeah. I forgot that part. After she *killed* me, Bandit attacked and bit Lynn on the back of the leg. She screamed and tried to kick him, but he cloaked himself. Lynn missed. After she rushed to the kitchen to grab a towel, she sat on the sofa. That was when she delivered her tirade about being happy that she'd killed me."

I took another slug of coffee. "That is amazing. You guys are the best."

"Who's going to play Alexa now?" Rihanna asked. "Or will the studio cancel the movie?"

"Good question."

A knock sounded on our office door, and a moment later, Steve poked his head in. "I thought I saw you all come in here. Mind if I join you?"

"Of course not. Genevieve was just filling me in on what happened."

"Can I get you some coffee?" Jaxson asked.

"That would be great."

I don't know why he always accepted coffee from Jaxson but not from me—unless I was waitressing.

He sat down. "If Genevieve filled you in on how she was *murdered*, I'll mention that the people from the other prison arrived and have arrested Lynn. We no longer have to worry about being threatened."

"That is so great," I said.

Steve looked over at Hugo. "Thanks to the big guy here. He is very good at wearing a camera and keeping the subject in frame."

Hugo smiled and nodded.

"He says thank you," Genevieve responded.

"Have you spoken with Shawn?" I asked.

Jaxson placed a fresh cup of coffee on the table for Steve. "I did. He was upset at first, but we all believe that the movie can return full speed ahead now."

"Who will play Alexa?" Rihanna asked.

"Actually, Lisa Pena will."

I smiled. "I liked her. I'm sure her brother had a say in that, but good for both of them."

Steve sipped the coffee. "Once more, I couldn't have done this without my magical team behind me. So, thank you."

"It was our pleasure. I'll be glad when this movie is over. I'm rather tired of redoing the same diner scene over and over again."

"I'm sure you are." After he gulped down the rest of the brew, he stood. "Thanks again."

Once Steve left, a swell of satisfaction washed over me. "We did it—or rather our dynamic duo here did it." Bandit lifted up on his two back feet. "I mean our dynamic trio."

"You better believe it," he said.

"Speaking of Bandit, Hugo would like me to call Valerie, Janet's sister, and ask if Bandit can stay with us," Genevieve said.

"Define *us*." I said.

"Hugo and me. We really would like to be foster parents."

"I love that idea," I said. Iggy would be exceptionally happy.

Rihanna finished her drink, but held it in her hand. "In that case, I would like to propose a new idea."

"What's that?" I asked.

"If Genevieve and Hugo are going to be parents, I think Hugo should be given a last name."

That was a wonderful idea. "What do you suggest?"

"I think Hugo should decide. I know Genevieve picked his first name, but he must have an idea what he'd like for a last name," my cousin said.

Hugo smiled and then told Genevieve. "Really? Hemingway. Hmm. I think it's a wonderful last name." She turned to us. "You probably don't know this, but Hugo loves to read, and Ernest Hemingway is one of his favorite authors."

"No kidding. I suppose if he stays in the Hex and Bones back room most of the time, he needs something to do."

I lifted my now empty coffee cup. "To Hugo Hemingway, bodyguard and truth extractor extraordinaire."

Iggy crawled out of Hugo's grasp and up to his shoulder. When he pressed his snout to Hugo's cheek, my heart melted. Our family seemed quite complete—at least for now.

. . .

Don't forget to sign up for my Cozy Mystery newsletter *to learn about my discounts and upcoming releases. If you prefer to only receive notices regarding my releases, follow me on BookBub.*

THE END

ABOUT VELLA DAY

Love it HOT and STEAMY? Sign up for my newsletter and receive MONTANA DESIRE for FREE. Click here

OR Are you a fan of quirky PARANORMAL COZY MYSTERIES? Sign up for this newsletter. Click Here

Not only do I love to read, write, and dream, I'm an extrovert. I enjoy being around people and am always trying to understand what makes them tick. Not only must my romance books have a happily ever after, I need characters I can relate to. My men are wonderful, dynamic, smart, strong, and the best lovers in the world (of course).

My Paranormal Cozy Mysteries are where I let my imagination run wild with witches and a talking pink iguana who believes he's a real sleuth.

I believe I am the luckiest woman. I do what I love and I have a wonderful, supportive husband, who happens to be hot!

Fun facts about me

(1) I'm a math nerd who loves spreadsheets. Give me numbers and I'll find a pattern.

(2) I live on a Costa Rica beach!

(3) I also like to exercise. Yes, I know I'm odd.

I love hearing from readers either on FB or via email (hint, hint).

Social Media Sites

Website: www.velladay.com

FB: www.facebook.com/vella.day.90

Twitter: velladay4

Gmail: velladayauthor@gmail.com

ALSO BY VELLA DAY

A WITCH'S COVE MYSTERY (Paranormal Cozy Mystery)

PINK Is The New Black (book 1)

A PINK Potion Gone Wrong (book 2)

The Mystery of the PINK Aura (book 3)

Box Set (books 1-3)

Sleuthing In The PINK (book 4)

Not in The PINK (book 5)

Gone in the PINK of an Eye (book 6)

Box Set (books 4-6)

The PINK Pumpkin Party (book 7)

Mistletoe with a PINK Bow (book 8)

The Magical PINK Pendant (book 9)

The Poisoned PINK Punch (book 10)

PINK Smoke and Mirrors (book 11)

Broomsticks and PINK Gumdrops (book 12)

Knotted Up In PINK Yarn (book 13)

Ghosts and PINK Candles (book 14)

Pilfering The PINK Pearls (book 15)

The Case of The Stolen PINK Tombstone (book 16)

The PINK Christmas Cookie Caper (book 17)

PINK Moon Rising (book 18)

SILVER LAKE SERIES (3 OF THEM)

(1). <u>**HIDDEN REALMS OF SILVER LAKE**</u>
(Paranormal Romance)

Awakened By Flames (book 1)

Seduced By Flames (book 2)

Kissed By Flames (book 3)

Destiny In Flames (book 4)

Box Set (books 1-4)

Passionate Flames (book 5)

Ignited By Flames (book 6)

Touched By Flames (book 7)

Box Set (books 5-7)

Bound By Flames (book 8)

Fueled By Flames (book 9)

Scorched By Flames (book 10)

(2). <u>**FOUR SISTERS OF FATE: HIDDEN
REALMS OF SILVER LAKE**</u> (Paranormal Romance)

Poppy (book 1)

Primrose (book 2)

Acacia (book 3)

Magnolia (book 4)

Box Set (books 1-4)

Jace (book 5)

Tanner (book 6)

(3). **WERES AND WITCHES OF SILVER LAKE**

(Paranormal Romance)

A Magical Shift (book 1)

Catching Her Bear (book 2)

Surge of Magic (book 3)

The Bear's Forbidden Wolf (book 4)

Her Reluctant Bear (book 5)

Freeing His Tiger (book 6)

Protecting His Wolf (book 7)

Waking His Bear (book 8)

Melting Her Wolf's Heart (book 9)

Her Wolf's Guarded Heart (book 10)

His Rogue Bear (book 11)

Box Set (books 1-4)

Box Set (books 5-8)

Reawakening Their Bears (book 12)

OTHER PARANORMAL SERIES

PACK WARS (Paranormal Romance)

Training Their Mate (book 1)

Claiming Their Mate (book 2)

Rescuing Their Virgin Mate (book 3)

Box Set (books 1-3)

Loving Their Vixen Mate (book 4)

Fighting For Their Mate (book 5)

Enticing Their Mate (book 6)

Box Set (books 1-4)

Complete Box Set (books 1-6)

HIDDEN HILLS SHIFTERS (Paranormal Romance)

An Unexpected Diversion (book 1)

Bare Instincts (book 2)

Shifting Destinies (book 3)

Embracing Fate (book 4)

Promises Unbroken (book 5)

Bare 'N Dirty (book 6)

Hidden Hills Shifters Complete Box Set (books 1-6)

CONTEMPORARY SERIES

MONTANA PROMISES (Full length contemporary Romance)

Promises of Mercy (book 1)

Foundations For Three (book 2)

Montana Fire (book 3)

Montana Promises Box Set (books 1-3)

Hart To Hart (Book 4)

Burning Seduction (Book 5)

Montana Promises Complete Box Set (books 1-5)

<u>ROCK HARD, MONTANA</u> (contemporary romance novellas)

Montana Desire (book 1)

Awakening Passions (book 2)

<u>PLEDGED TO PROTECT</u> (contemporary romantic suspense)

From Panic To Passion (book 1)

From Danger To Desire (book 2)

From Terror To Temptation (book 3)

Pledged To Protect Box Set (books 1-3)

<u>BURIED SERIES</u> (contemporary romantic suspense)

Buried Alive (book 1)

Buried Secrets (book 2)

Buried Deep (book 3)

The Buried Series Complete Box Set (books 1-3)

A NASH MYSTERY (Contemporary Romance)

Sidearms and Silk(book 1)

Black Ops and Lingerie(book 2)

A Nash Mystery Box Set (books 1-2)

STARTER SETS (Romance)

Contemporary

Paranormal

Printed in Great Britain
by Amazon

76063451R00144